LIFE IN
GOD'S HANDS

ABIOLA OLOJO

P.O. Box 402

Swiftwater, PA 18370

(973) 348-5067

sspublishingcompany@gmail.com

www.sharsheypublishingcompany.com

Copyright © 2021 Abiola Olojo

ISBN-13: 978-1-7348030-9-9

Publisher: Shar- Shey Publishing Company LLC

Book Cover Designed by: Adeola Disu

Edited by: Nicole Reed

PRAISE FOR THE BOOK

This book is a book of hope, against all odds. It is a book that will help you learn about how to navigate through hard days and dark hours, and even after getting lost in the gloomy clouds of life, knowing fully well that all your life is in God's hands will help you find solace and comfort.

-Pastor Bose Adelaja,
God Embassy Church, Ukraine

I'm highly honoured and privileged to review this life-changing memo of yours. I have benefited so much as a person by going through the entire book and I strongly believe that it will be a great addition to other books in this subject. I pray that this book will be a blessing to whoever reads it. Amen.

-Yours in Christ
Caleb

This book was definitely worth the read. I enjoyed the fact that it was from a perspective of someone who has actually been through life challenges and suffered from a loss of a loved one. It shows people that they are not alone when it comes to dealing with life problems.

-Adeshina Abiona

The author, professes that, our tomorrow will always be better than today if we have a determined mind, aspire towards a better tomorrow seeking

God's favour through prayers, instead of crying over spilt milk. Your attitude she says will surely bring you to a new altitude that will separate you from the multitude. I have read this book and I am certain, that the readers will benefit immensely and learn a lot of lessons that will improve their lives. I sincerely recommend this book.

-Dapo Abudu ESQ.

This book gives the exact picture of how a life can succeed in God's hands despite difficulties and challenges of life. It is a go-to recipe for anyone who wants to win at life.

-Sam Owoeye, MD

WORDS FROM HER CHILDREN

Several years ago, Abiola Olojo and her children went through a tragedy in the loss of her husband and our father- Joshua Olojo. However, in spite of this, she rose and did great things in honor of her loving late husband and our dad.

Abiola Olojo, my mom, is not only a mother to me, but to the world. Her love and compassion for changing this world for the better is what makes me proud to say that I am her son. In addition to this, her strength and qualities of being a virtuous woman make me to love her even more and is what I hope to find in a future wife as well.

To whomever reads this book, you are in for lots of excitement, a time of learning and a time of meditation in God's word and I pray it blesses you just as my mom Abiola Olojo has been a blessing to me.

-Ayodeji Odulaja

This has been a highly anticipated day for our family. Our beloved mom, Abiola Olojo, is officially releasing her book! This book creates a special connection between Abiola and the audience of widows and those who are actively battling dilemmas in life. In addition, the knowledge the book provides comes from raw experiences and truth. I couldn't be more excited for people to get their hands on this book. This is an exceptional read! We, as a family, are so proud of you, mom!

-Dapo Olojo

My mother is so strong, and her strength, wisdom, and compassion encompasses day to day existence. This book is filled with nuggets of sagacity and knowledge that you will be able to use during hardships that life tends to throw our way. Your thought process will not be the same after reading this book. Thank you, mom, for writing this book to help others heal while you yourself are healing.

-Abisola Olojo

CONTENTS

ACKNOWLEDGMENTS

I thank everyone who has been of great blessings in my life. I thank all my children (both biological and adopted) for their unwavering love and support all the time. You guys know *Mommy loves you.* I thank God for my husband, (of blessed memory), who lived a worthy and exemplary life; till we meet again at the feet of Christ, where we will meet to part no more. And to my husband's bosom friend, Lawyer Abudu, thanks so much sir for being an inspiration to my family. I thank my parents, my brother and sisters, my friends and all well-wishers. I thank Dr. Sunday Adelaja for being a blessing to me. I pray may we all continue to grow and flourish in Christ. I love you all.

DEDICATION

To my darling husband, Joshua Olojo (of blessed memory), the one who taught me love and value through patience. Continue to sleep in the bosom of our Lord Jesus Christ. Love you!

PROLOGUE

I have known the author, Mrs Abiola Olojo since she was born and being a close first cousin, I have had the privilege of following her life profile from childhood to the present day.

Her parental upbringing, humble lifestyle, kindheartedness before and after the loss of her dutiful husband and her Christian persuasion with energy speak volumes, of which this book is an example. Indeed, she confirms in the book that the loving spirit of her husband which still sustains her is the propelling force behind writing this book.

Given the various challenges that life has thrown at her, I wish to congratulate her that even at almost 60, she is able to gather her thoughts together to write a book which I consider a must read for an average person seeking surveyor through trust and confidence in God and determined efforts to make success in life.

Abiola's ability to weave words in an enchanting way, and quoting relevant scriptures to back her sentiments, arguments and suppositions on the pattern of life to adopt makes the book one of the best that one can find in shaping one's pattern of life.

Her choice of words and expressions has a way of sending the message home in a clear and precise manner, thereby keeping the reader glued to his seat till he gets to the last page of the concluding chapter.

'LIFE IN GOD'S HAND' mirrors the life of an average person facing monumental challenges leading to self-delusion. The book makes references to Biblical and true live examples of people whose strength of character and purpose driven efforts yielded desired dividends.

Giving her various personal testimonies through a glimpse into her past, and current experience as a widow woman, she is able to drive home her point to any woman with her label and heart.

Although she is not an ordained Pastor the author proved with an available quotation from the scriptures that a believer enjoys the riches and good qualities of divine grace in full abundance and to the utmost extent of his needs. Nothing can be more gratifying than one's life being refreshed and quickened by divine grace.

Using her own life experience, she went further to establish that the believer must regard Christ as a luxurious delicacy and a rare and exquisite delight. For a life of ultimate goals, he must submit cheerfully and totally to the sovereignty of God. He must think of His mighty love which drew him to die on the cross and see him as risen, crowned and glorified.

The author advised she had an encounter with God's spirit after her husband's death. She believes God created her to help people and cannot afford to see anyone suffer and take her eyes off. In fulfillment of the foregoing, she has found peace, Joy and satisfaction which overcome distress and difficulties in her life.

In the last two chapters, she directed attention to the social needs and problems of the average person, and social relationships, emphasizing the need for Love for God and for one another. Everyone is created to be a blessing to the world. The truth is that life is a gift from God, and he wants us to use it for His purpose. Her loss and sufferings constitute a platform from which she is witnessing for Christ, so vigorously and transparently that her love for God and man is visible. I pray that with much grace, upholding and humility, her witnessing will be to her Master's glory, Amen.

I wish to recommend this soul lifting book to the great and the small, the jubilant and the discouraged and indeed to all categories of men.

ENGR. ADEYINKA ODUKOYA

FOREWORD

Life in God's hand is an amazing blessing from God, looking at the content of the book but also looking at the writer of the book. Having the privilege of knowing Mrs Abiola Olojo, her story and her life, I am personally overwhelmed by the transformation I have seen her go through in just a few years since I have come to know her. The first time I saw her, she was a lady in sorrow going through the loss of her husband, but three years later, she has turned her sorrow into her platform.

To everyone that is going to read this book, I want to tell you that you are reading a book that isn't just theory. This is a book by somebody who has experienced it all and knows what she is talking about. This lady in my own eyes is of the same calibre and quality as Mother Teresa. But starting at the time she did and from where she started to a place of releasing this book, all my respect and admiration goes to her.

I want to encourage everybody to help themselves by getting a hold of this book.

Dr Sunday Adelaja
Senior Pastor Embassy of God Church, Kyiv Ukraine.

INTRODUCTION

Hardly is there no time things are not happening around us or within us. We wake up every day to see the light of a new day and have expectations for the day. As we get set for the day, thousands of thoughts run through our minds. Some produce fear, some give us confidence, and others make us worry and make our hearts beat faster. It could be about some projects that we have not completed, or some meetings that are on our schedule, or some protracted problems that have denied any form of solutions we've ever attempted, and so on. We almost cannot avoid one of these. Situations come from time to time to scrutinize our faith and confidence in whatsoever we keep in our hearts. But it will be a different ball game to understand that our life, from the beginning to the end is in the hands of the one who created it. *"Life in God's hands"* is a phrase that gives us all the confidence and assurance that we need to run the journey of life without fear whatsoever. You may not be sure if your life is in your father's or mother's hands, or your friend or any of your loved ones' hands, but it's in God's hands. That gives you the boldness and courage to face all of the life situations and challenges. What about if somebody threatens you with death? You have overcome the fear of death, and all forms of insecurities. Why? *Because your life is secured and insured in God.* You can face your business and do your work with all the peace and rest of mind available in this world. Life becomes way easier when you know that there's someone in charge and has made all the provisions available. That's what you will find through the pages of this book. I'm not giving you a prophecy; I'm only telling you what is real and what I've personally enjoyed and still enjoying in my life. I want you to go through this book with an open mind so that you can enjoy all the benefits therein. If you've ever experienced success in life, there are more that you are about to experience, and if not at all, you've come to that moment of change and turning point in your life. You will surely manifest all that you are created for and see how beautiful and glorious your life is and will continue to be as you keep working and believing. I welcome you to a new order of living and believing. *My regards.*

Abiola Olojo
May 2021

ABOUT THE BOOK

Every day, we are cumbered with loads of care and concerns for life. I have seen God faithful in all His doings, even when they seem unclear to us. Life becomes way easier to live when we know it is already in His hands and allow His plan to work in our plans.

In this book, you will find.

- New perspectives to what life is all about,

- What it means for a life to be in God's hands, and

- How things that happen to us can be turned to our advantage, as I shared my own life experiences and ideas.

CHAPTER 1
LOST BUT FOUND

"Bros Joe, what made you think God will not give you the opportunity you need. In fact, he's already done; He gave you a good life and a wonderful family. And whatever plans we have, let's trust him. He will surely make all good, even now and beyond."

-Abiola Olojo, while talking with her husband

(of blessed memory)

A dreadful day it was!!! the 11th of September 2001 (known as 9/11 in America), Islamist terrorists hijacked four planes that were flying above the US. Two of them were flown into the twin towers of the World Trade Center in New York. Another was crashed into the Pentagon, the top military building in the capital city, Washington DC, and the fourth was crashed into a field in Stonycreek Township near Shanksville, Pennsylvania. The attack shocked the world. It was the biggest terrorist attack ever on America. My husband who worked in one of the Twin towers came into the building a few minutes later than the normal time he would have been in his office. As he strode a few meters towards the elevator, he noticed something was going on as everywhere was chaotic and the Emergency Service was hauling everyone out of the building. Not long after, the building collapsed, and everyone took to their heels. He managed to escape but inhaled some of the noxious fumes and particles that came out of the explosion. I was at work when the news broke, and I had to rush home. Right there at home, I was watching how the ugly incident happened. I wouldn't believe my eyes. I thought my husband would have been in his office at the time of the incident. Fear gripped me and I became apprehensive and unrestful. All the emergency numbers we were given to call were busy and there wasn't any way I could reach him. He later called with someone's phone and I tried to call him back but couldn't reach him. With my children, my siblings and everyone around me, I couldn't wait to see him. When he eventually came, we all leaped for joy. Then, he told the story of how the incident happened. We couldn't believe our ears. We just thanked God he came back home safely. And what a day! A day we would never forget in our lives. Then, later, he went to the hospital for checkups and was put on close monitoring.

DIAGNOSIS WAS MADE

After several monitoring and checkups, some findings were made. Some of the noxious fumes and particles he inhaled at the incident had affected his lungs. And as treatments continued, the damage became more malignant. I had to leave everything else I was doing to face my husband. I gave him all the attention and support he needed. The situation was overwhelming, but I trusted God and believed everything would be fine. So, I endured all the stress and rigor I had to go through.

EVERY WAY, GOD WINS

In all things, God wins. Times when all hope is lost and you don't know what next step to take or do, in such situations, God wins. Even when it seems you've been defeated and lost to the battle of life, God wins. He's winning in you and through you. You will see and know that there's nothing too late for him to do. Is there anything you think you've lost, you will find it, this time around, *more*. If it's joy you've lost, you will find more. If it's peace of mind, happiness, success, love, support, care, and all the good things of life and great people in your life, that you have lost, I tell you, you will find more. Look at this; *In all these things we are more than conquerors through him who loves us and died for us.* That tells us that in all the things we've gone through or going through, we are more than conquerors. In other words, we have the assurance of victory, not by ourselves, but by God, our father who loves us and fought the battle on our behalf. There are many battles of life that we cannot fight on our own. But in those times, we've found solace and help in God at every time of need.

AND WE LOST HIM

On that day, I got the news that my husband is dead. Gently, in disbelief, I said *"no, it's not possible! My husband cannot die!!!* I don't mean spiritual death, but physical death. Because I had all the sense of assurance that he would survive the sickness. I'd just like to say this that -in everything we go through, we should trust God, not just for miracles, but for something much more important- *His love. His love never fails, even if every other thing does.* On that day, calls flooded my phone that I'd never seen before, from early morning till night and I received all. People around me told me to go rest but I insisted I'm fine and answered all the calls. It was still like a dream in the night. Every way, I thank God for the people around me who supported and went out of their ways to stay with me and comfort me. May they be blessed some more.

I'M FOREVER GRATEFUL

One decision I was always happy I made was marrying my husband, who was the love of my life and an amazing father to his children. There are so many nice things to say about him. He was such a hardworking and godly man. To lose such a person is devastating. It was like my whole world was coming to an end, but I had God with me and I had to be strong for my children. I remember what my children said about him. They said, *"We are grateful that God gave our father 15 years more to live with us after the September 11 incident that took away many lives for instance. It was indeed a great and memorable time for us to know our father more and learn a lot from him."* And I thanked God He gave them the opportunity to know their father. Many things they are doing now came from the things they have learned from their father. He was such a blessing. Many things happened after his death-from what I had to deal with inside to what I had to deal with outside. I saw different things. Some were good. Some weren't. All in all, I've learned to thank God. There were moments when I would cry profusely and want to give up, but when I remembered my husband's words, my heart was consoled. Then when he was still alive, he would say "I should not cry, and be strong for our children." Though he was on the sickbed, he never once complained about anything but always grateful to God for everything he had received. All that challenged me and made me summon the courage to trust God more and stand strong for my children. And worthy of note, are people who God has raised to help me. I don't feel lonely because I know I have God and His people. That for me is a great blessing.

WHAT HAVE YOU LOST?

Aaron Moser was seventeen years old when tragedy struck during a 1998 local junior league hockey game in British Columbia. He was checked into the boards, hit his headfirst, and broke his neck. Initially it seemed it was something minor that could easily be handled, but later found out that the injury had caused Aaron his spinal cord to be damaged, leaving him a quadriplegic, with all his limbs; arms and legs completely paralyzed. He had no feelings or movement below his chest because all the nerves were severely damaged. For Aaron who was such an athletic and active guy, who was popular among his mates, it was a brutal blow. For his family, they had to adapt to the sad situation and give him all the care and support he needed and helped him to adjust to his new life. This also had to go with extra expenses and sacrifice. To get around this situation, his family, friends, and the entire community set up a trust fund to cover supplies, equipment, wheelchair, renovations, and other expenses. Not long enough, the trust fund was swamped with donations- not just from people in the area who knew Aaron, but also from people throughout the world of hockey. The people weren't just motivated by the tragedy; they were inspired by the way the teenager handled the shocking change to his life. Aaron refused to complain or condemn anybody for his fate. He surmounted undaunted courage that made him keep working hard and long enough to walk again. The trust fund established on his behalf kept attracting more and more donations. After a while, there was enough money, not only to help Aaron but also to set up a foundation in his name —a non-profit organization dedicated to helping find a cure for him and others with spinal cord injuries. What happened to Aaron has opened doors of treatments for others who are also in the same situations and have hopes for a better future.

FROM RASHES TO GLORY (TEMPORARY LOST, PERMANENT FOUND)

The first time I read her story, I was blown away. Hardly is there anyone in the account of the history of the world who has risen so far to such a high level of wealth and influence from a ground bottom of abject poverty as she has done. She was born by a single teenage mother. Her assumed father left her mother not long after a single sexual encounter that led to her conception. Her mother was a housemaid. After the birth, her mother traveled north and left her in the hands of her grandmother. She lived in abject poverty and was so poor that she often wore dresses made of potato sacks, and children in the neighborhood would come and make jest of her. Her grandmother taught her to read before the age of three and took her to the local church, where she was nicknamed as *'The Preacher'* for being a brilliant young girl who recites Bible verses every time. She later moved and went to stay with her mother, who gave birth to another daughter around that time. However, as her mother was having difficulties taking care of her and her younger sister, she was sent to live with the man she would call her father, Vernon. Initially, she had been sexually molested by her cousin when she was nine years old. And at age 13, she ran away from home after several sufferings. When she was 14, she became pregnant and delivered a son, but her son was born prematurely and died shortly after birth. She got involved with drugs and emotionally abusive men. But she wouldn't give up on her dreams. She had a spirit that would not be destroyed. She puts all her hurtful experiences in the past and is determined to learn, grow and succeed in life. She became a top student in high school, won public-speaking contests and the state beauty pageant. She won a full university scholarship and came out with a first degree in Communication. Her first job was working at a local grocery store. Her big break came when she got an offer from a local radio station. She puts in all her best and it wasn't long before her hard work and talent would earn her a spot in television news. She got so involved in her stories, and sometimes became so emotional with her guests during her talk shows. She took the TV talk show to another level. And before anyone knew it, it has become the number one spotlight in the city, and the top-rated spot in the entire nation. Within a few years, her show had gained the highest number of viewers of any talk show all over the world. And she was on her way to launching a series of successful TV and radio shows, magazines, websites, charities, and the world's most influential book club. She was a millionaire in her thirties, and before you know it, she became a billionaire. She's often described as one of the most powerful women in the world, and one of the greatest philanthropists of all time. I'm sure by now, you must have guessed right who I'm sharing her story. She is Oprah Winfrey. She came from the rock bottom of life to a high level of wealth and significance. Is there anything you think you've lost in your life? Or maybe it's your detestable past that is meddling with your present. Dust away your past and begin to work on your future. If nothing could stop Oprah from achieving her goals in life, nothing can stop you.

DIFFICULT TO EXPRESS

How is it? That sometimes, it's difficult to express our feelings, talk to someone or just even open our mouth. Perhaps it could be an accumulation of stress or one of those moments when we feel overwhelmed by what we go through. The feeling comes more often than not, and at such moments, we just want to give up all and have at least some rest, maybe a lasting one. The troubles and difficulties are just so much that we don't even know who to talk to or who can solve our problem or really understand what we go through. So, these are what we feel, and a lot of times, they meddle with our decisions and cloud our judgment. But how do we go through this? How do we handle them and bring out a good solution? First, I want you to understand that no matter how personal or private the feelings and situations might be, they are what some of us have gone through. It's not your fault to have those feelings and experience. But here's what you can do. You know our feelings are important. They make us relate and connect with the world around and within us. But they are never our life. When we have such feelings, we'd think the world would come to an end, but no, it won't. They are temporary, just for the moment. *So, don't make a permanent decision in a temporary situation.* Find somewhere to relax and rest your mind. At those moments, God is closer to you than you would ever imagine. Pay attention to His spirit in you. He will give you peace and comfort. Direct you in the way you should go. Sometimes we could have stress or anxieties that we've accumulated over a period of time. At those moments, we could have some rest, or if we want to go out, meet with our friends or go for recreational activities, to relax our body and mind.

HERE IS THE FACT

Death brings us to fulfillment. Death brings us to rest. Our spirit never dies, but our body does. We are not our body, but spirit. Our body is the case that houses our spirit on earth. So, when our body dies, our spirit remains alive. Our spirit is from God, but our body is from the earth. Let's look at how our body is formed. According to Biology, we understood that fertilization of sperm and ovum forms zygote. Zygote grows into an embryo and embryo into a fetus. The fetus becomes matured and is delivered as a baby, a small human. The small human begins to feed and grow, and eventually becomes an adult human. The feeding consists of food that is obtained from plants and animals. Plants get their nutrients from the soil. Animals get their nutrients from plants. So, man indirectly gets his nutrients from the soil. And since food forms the body, man's body is from the earth. And so, while on earth, the body should be used for the benefit of the earth and the glory of God. The earth is given to us. Your body is given to us. So, we must use our body to the glory of God, and the benefits of mankind. If you have talent with your voice, hands, legs, brain, or whole-body, Use it. Let it be a blessing to people, and that would make you memorable on earth and people would continue to celebrate you, even long after you've gone.

HOW TO OVERCOME THE FEAR OF DEATH

I know fear is part of human instinct. It informs us and shields us away from whatever we may perceive as a threat or danger to our life. Be that as it may, fear of death is unique. Let's imagine a scenario; someone suddenly came out of nowhere and raised a gun over someone, threatening to kill that person, if that was the first time the person had that experience, he could probably pee on himself or feel like his heart would come out of his mouth.

It's that terrifying. The fear could be so strong that the person may even go into a coma. Now, what's this whole fear all about? It's the fear of death. The fear of whatever can terminate one's life. Our life is sacred, and nature has put that desire in everyone to always run away from whatever that can put that life in danger. This is common to all creatures. But to overcome the fear of death when you are not endangering your life is to know that death is a transition. Like I mentioned earlier, death doesn't kill you. It only separates you from your body and transfers you to the other side. So, when you are occupied with your purpose and things you have to do here on earth, you don't bother yourself with the fear of death. Those who commit suicide have got something wrong in their system. They've become overwhelmed and inundated with problems that it has suppressed the fear of taking their lives. They thought they would rather feel better when they are not alive than to keep living and continue to see their problems and difficulties. But what they wouldn't know is that there's always hope ahead. There are always better days ahead. Despite the difficulties and challenges now, things would get better. What we just need to do is to keep a good attitude. If you are in a situation or someone you know is in a situation and they are already thinking of committing suicide or giving up on life, please help me tell them, -one thing is certain, beyond all manner of doubt, that there's hope ahead. There's joy in the future. Whatever may look difficult now, will soon be easy. No condition is permanent is what we always say, and that is true. And because you believe and begin to work in line of your belief, things will change for good, and much more, *for better*.

THE DEPTH OF A MOTHER'S LOVE

One summer afternoon, a young mother laid her baby girl to sleep in her cradle. She said to herself "I'll just go to meet one of my friends in the neighborhood for a minute or so to visit. I haven't had time to talk with her for such a long time. But while she and her friend were having their ladies talk, the city fire alarm sent a chill through them both. "Don't worry," said her friend. "Most likely it's only a grass fire. There are lots of them at this time of year. I'm sure the fire isn't anywhere near here." "But listen," said the mother. "I think I hear the fire engine coming this way. Look! People are running down the street-running toward my house!" Without another word, she dashed into the street and ran with the gathering crowd. Then she saw it. Her own house was on fire! Smoke and flames were already pouring through the roof. "My baby!" she cried frantically. "My baby!" The crowd was thick around the house, but she pushed and shoved until she reached the door. A fireman stopped her and said, "You can't go in there! You will be burned!" But the mother cried, "Let me go! Let me go!" as she broke free and dashed into the flaming house. She knew just where to go. Running through the smoke and

flames, she seized her precious baby, then turned
to make her way out. But by now the smoke made
it very hard to see and breathe. Nearly overcome,
she swayed and fell, and would not have made it
out of the house safely if a fireman had not picked
her up and carried her out. What a cheer went up as
they appeared! Baby Marjorie was not hurt at all!
But the poor mother's hands were terribly burned.
Kind friends took care of the baby while the ambu-
lance took her to the hospital. The doctors did their
best, but her hands were terribly scared. Years later, when Marjorie had grown, she suddenly noticed
something she had not noticed before. Her mother's
hands were so ugly! "Why are your hands so ugly?"
she asked her mother when they were alone. Tears
filled her mother's eyes as she remembered how
frightened she was the day the house burned with
Marjorie asleep and unaware of the danger. "Have
I said something wrong?" Marjorie asked when she
saw the tears. "No, my dear," replied her mother.
"But there's a story I need to tell you." Then she
told Marjorie the story of the fire. She told how the
people tried to hold her back, how the fireman tried
to stop her, how she battled the flames to rescue
her, how she fell, and how they were rescued. Then
she held out her scarred hands for Marjorie to see.
"They are ugly, in a way, aren't they," Mother said
softly. "For me, the only thing that mattered was to
save your life." Now it was Marjorie's turn to shed a
few tears. "Oh, Mother," she cried, "You must love
me so much! These are the most beautiful hands in

all the world!" Do you know there are hands that were hurt for you? Do you know there's someone who suffered pains so you can have gains? At times we imagined the pains and stress that our parents, especially our mothers have gone through to take us to where we are today. How much love have we showed back to them? If we could and should be grateful to our parents for all they've done for us, how much more the one who gave his life for us, won't we appreciate and honor him? I'm absolutely sure that there's nothing else he wouldn't give if we'll believe and trust him for it.

YOU MAY HAVE GOOD OLD DAYS, BUT THERE ARE BETTER NEW DAYS

Oftentimes we experience Saudade. Saudade is the deep emotional feeling of nostalgia towards the absence of a loved one or something in the past. It is the love, feelings, emotions, memories or thoughts that remain after someone we love or situation has passed. Many times we attach to the past, that we don't want to live in the present and enjoy the blessings of the future. There are definitely going to be certain moments we loved and cherished either alone or with someone and we wouldn't mind having those moments again, but the truth is -there are better days ahead, only if we can leave the past so that we can enjoy the future. Beyond the good, there's always the better. But if we cling to the good, we will not see the better. We might think we've reached the height of enjoyment in life until we have a new experience and realize there are always better days ahead. Though things might be hard and situations difficult to cope with, I promise you that your attitude will surely bring you to a new *altitude that will separate you from the multitude.* We hardly believe there's something better when we lose someone/something precious to us. But not until we believe and begin to experience it for ourselves. This is not to make us not feel remorseful or grieve over our loved ones, but it is to assure us that *our past can never be better than our future.* There are always new things ahead of the old things that we might have experienced. The old life can never be better than the new life if we have a new mind. We've got to imbibe a new mind. A new mind helps us to generate new thoughts. New thoughts set the atmosphere for new life. New mind comes from exposing ourselves to new information, new knowledge and new ideas that are capable of transforming our minds and giving us fresh wisdom. Situations and things around us don't have names, we give them names. It's the name we give them that they answer to. It doesn't matter whether they presented themselves good or bad to us. They are all the same. A situation somebody called *opportunity* is the same situation that another person called a problem. The difference is in the naming, not the situation. What you call any situation is what it answers to you. If you call a problem, you will see a problem. If you call opportunity, you will see opportunity. Next time you are faced with any situation, decide the name you want to give that situation and it will answer to you as you have named it. There's always opportunity to learn new things in life. *Nothing is a waste, only if we know how to use it.*

WHERE HAPPINESS COMES FROM

Different things make different people happy. Someone can be happy now and in the next minute become sad. But where does happiness come from? Is it what we can control or keep with us? I will answer that in a minute. Happiness is more about what we do than what people do to us. If people do good to us, we are happy. But if they do otherwise, we are unhappy. But it takes wisdom to understand that happiness essentially has nothing to do with what people do to us, but everything to do with what we do to ourselves and others. When God created us, he puts all that we'll need to enjoy life right inside of us. Happiness comes when we do what we love to do. What we love to do is engraved in our being. It's in our nature and design. When we do it, we function well and become happy. An electric iron is happy ironing clothes because that's what it's designed to do, not for boiling water or cooking food because it has a hot surface. Many of us are not doing what we are supposed to do and we expect happiness. That's not possible. That's why sometimes we are frustrated and overwhelmed. We could feel some emptiness or voidness inside. That's because we are not doing what we are supposed to do. Some people can decide to run after money and forsake happiness. After getting the money, then they will start looking for happiness. They think money will make them happy. But that's not. Money does not bring happiness if we are not happy before. The concept of money has been grossly misunderstood. Money is a tool that must not be idolized. It's an essential tool but not the only tool. So, we've got to set our priorities right and understand the important things of life. We'll discuss that much later. So, happiness comes from doing what we are created to do, and that's what we love to do, and that's what we can do without money, and that's what we do to add value to humanity.

BURNING OF KING'S HOUSE ADDS MORE VALUE TO IT

Perhaps you've lost something/someone valuable to you, and you think you can't have anything as valuable as them, I got you. Here is the thing- whatever or whoever is so precious to you is precious because there's something good in them or about them. If you lost your spouse- husband or wife, and you both loved each other. The pain of losing a partner would be so much that it would really take some time to heal. Yes, I know I've had the experience as well. Now, here is the truth, God in us is sweeter than the sweetest one we've ever known on earth. Let me explain- Do you know God is good? He's not only good but gives out His goodness. And His goodness is always new every morning. If you think you know anything about God, be ready to know Him afresh this year. He will show you new goodness, kindness, and love that will supersede what you've ever known about him. For us as humans, if we lived with someone long enough, we can predict almost everything they can do. We can tell how they talk, think or act; maybe not all the time, but most times. But when it comes to God, he's ever new and different. You would think you've known everything about God until he comes up with something that will blow your mind. You would think you'd come to the end of the road until a way just showed up from nowhere that you would wonder where it came from, because he, himself is the way. He brings forth water out of the desert and creates a way in the wilderness. If you know desert very well, you will know the last thing that you would expect is water, because there's dry and hot land everywhere and the soil is deep down far from the water table, so you won't bother to expect water in such an area. He said he's the water of life. When Israelites were so thirsty and almost dying, he became water for them that came out of the rock. Those are situations you know it's practically impossible to get a solution but he became the solution. He's the way. Anywhere you need the way and you believe him, he'll create the way. He's the water of life. Anywhere you are thirsty and have this dryness and drought in your life, he will fill and satisfy you. He makes things better. Whatever is lost in your life right now, he can give you back in multiple folds. He can restore all the loss, and renew your days as eagles', because he, himself is the restoration and resurrection. He will restore and resurrect all the lost and dead items in your life. I see you moving forward and upward.

CHAPTER 2
WHAT LIFE WOULD MEAN

"I'm no longer blind with religious stuff. I no longer worry about problems because I focus more on solutions. And I'm now a more grateful person than I was before and now love people more, even the unlovable."

-Abiola Olojo at 56

What would life mean to you? We've got several definitions and understandings about life, coupled with our own personal experiences and beliefs. But do you have a concrete definition of life? Sometimes we refer to life as a series of events, experiences, situations or circumstances that happen to us or people around us. And therein we found so many interesting and uninteresting things that both make us happy and unhappy. Would that be a definition of life? or maybe several stories that we've heard from people of how they lived their lives because of their decisions, convictions, and beliefs. This might be a little controversial but it's never. It's an understanding. Though there are many things in life, they wouldn't be enough to give a good definition of life. if someone is happy at the moment, he will say life is good. If another person is unhappy at the same moment, he will say life is unfair or cruel. But those are just circumstances. They are just situations that have got nothing to do with what life means. Let's take an illustration. If you are a student at a university and you are studying Medicine, you have many subjects you'll offer and a series of practicals and experiments that you would go through. Perhaps if we are to count the number of days, that would be a lot. But with all the activities and events that take place throughout your course of study, you will never call any of them medicine, though they are all in medicine, no single one of them is qualified to be called medicine. This is because they are all inside medicine, all the subjects, practicals, experiments, classes, activities, sports, events and so on. so next time when you are talking about life, you understand it's not just things that happen, neither is it people who experience those things but the entire structure in which all things consist and exist.

NOW, WHAT IS LIFE?

Life, first of all, is a gift. It is what every one of us receives without payment. Nobody ever bought the life they are living. All living things live life free of charge. If life could be bought, the rich would have bought extra lives, so that in case they exhaust the one they have, they can put in the extra ones. But that's not so. Every one of us is given this precious life to live and enjoy every day in one single lifetime. However, we have a different number of days to live that life on earth. Many times, we wished people who are close to us who have died had longer days to live here on earth with us. But the most beautiful thing is that we will still meet again. Life doesn't end here. They are not dead, they just moved to the other side, where there's no more sorrows, troubles or shame. Death came to take off their garment and transferred them to a place of rest. For as many of us that are still here on earth, let's appreciate and enjoy every moment we have with ourselves. Let's celebrate our spouse, children, siblings, relatives and everyone with us. This is a good time to appreciate ourselves, and thank God for the good life. The people you might not appreciate today, you might miss them tomorrow. Let's appreciate and celebrate people. Life is a gift and we are all given to live and enjoy it.

GROWING UP

Growing up, I found myself in a family of 6 children. My father was a schoolteacher, and my mother was a full housewife. My father gave me the name *"Abiola"* which means *"giving birth to wealth"* because it was that time that he got a job after searching for a long time. Just like any other person who would come from such an environment where I came from, I had a humble beginning. Despite this, our parents always desired and trained us to be diligent and work to the best of our abilities. We had several moments of struggles and we also used to observe both morning and evening devotions, and even at times when we were tired, we would still do it. We were absolutely devoted and committed to the things of God. Other children had to pay attention to us and see how we behave and do things because we were good models to them. As good and religious as our lives were then, I didn't have much understanding about what we were doing. I just knew this is what I learned from my parents and religious leaders, and I didn't have time for myself to understand those things, not until years later.

WHAT MY LIFE WOULD MEAN

I wouldn't want it complicated. But I would like it just as simple as it could be. Looking through my life, I may not know everything about myself but what I've heard people said about me over and over again is that I'm a quiet and loving person. They just love to be around me, sometimes for advice, sometimes for being cared for, or sometimes just for the fond of it. I understand God doesn't discriminate and he said he will not cast away whosoever comes to him. So, I can imagine that level of love and magnanimity and so what I can do is to reciprocate that same love to his people. When I go out of my way to help people, I understand what it means and why I'm doing it. It doesn't even matter whether people appreciate it or not. What matters is that I do it out of genuineness of my heart. I don't do things so that people can reward me back. I do things for people to express my nature and who I believe. People have complained to me severally that I give but I don't receive things from them. It's not arrogance or demeaning their gifts, but I just believe that instead of collecting gifts and stocking my shelves and wardrobes with many items, why shouldn't I give them to those who are in need. And that's what I encourage people who are close to me to do. If you have, give to those who don't have. They would appreciate you more than those who already have.

LIFE IS SERVICE

Albert Schweitzer was an Alsatian polymath. As a child, he showed talent for music. And later began to play for concerts and his music was loved by many. By the time he was a young man, he had become widely known and acknowledged as a world expert on building organs, interpreting classical music and making musical recordings. He made a good living with his music but wouldn't just settle for that. At age 30, he decided to give up his career and find more meaning in life. He realized there were a lot of people who he could help if he became a doctor. So, he went back to school. His family and friends thought he was crazy. After finishing medical school, he raised money from his music concerts to set off a healthcare facility in Gabon, where there was a critical shortage of medical care. He and his wife traveled a distance to achieve his goal. People came from hundreds of kilometers around to him and his wife for medical treatments. His hospital was the only one around and that most of the people had ever seen. Most times, he and his wife would work themselves to exhaustion. But incidentally, after a while, they were forced to stop when world war 1 broke out. After the war, Dr. Schweitzer went back to Gabon and rebuilt his abandoned hospital. He resumed his free medical care for all the people in that area and many of them flooded his place. For another forty years until his death, he spent most of his time in Gabon where he served the locals and attended to their health needs. He was awarded a Nobel Peace Prize for his humanitarian work, not just for his hospital work, but also for his personal philosophy of having Reference for Life. He had always advocated for respect for human life and everyone should respect others and recognize their right to life.

LIFE IS A JOURNEY

Can you remember the last journey you had? Perhaps you were inside a car. When the journey started and the car began to move, you noticed as the car was moving, you didn't move, you remained seated. Nothing essentially changed about you who is in the car, but at every moment in time, something is changing around the car, because it's on the move and so passing from one point to another. Now, picture your life as a moving car, where you were yesterday is different from where you are today. That's why you must make everyday count and matter in your life. We are on a journey and moving at every moment of life. But we also need to pay attention to the direction we are moving. Some people are moving their life in a wrong direction, while some in the right direction. What determines whether a life is moving the right or wrong direction? Or what determines whether a car is going the right or wrong direction? The destination. The driver knows first of all where he's going, then embarks on the journey. It's impossible to say a car is moving the right or wrong direction when you don't know where it's going. Destination gives direction. What is our destination? Our destination is who we should become, what we should achieve, and where we should be at the end of our journey here on earth. All these boils down to our purpose. Why we are here. If we know why we are here we will know what we are supposed to do. Sometimes we are confused about what we are supposed to do. But if we know first, why we are here- a question of purpose, then we will be able to answer the question of what we are supposed to do. First, there's a general purpose of why we are all here- to manage and beautify the earth, making heaven on earth. Second, there's a personal/individual purpose of why we are here. Out of the general purpose, there are individual purposes. All purposes are directed towards the betterment of humanity and the expansion of God's kingdom on earth. For instance, my purpose could be to focus on human health, then I can find my work in that direction, involving my passions, gifts, talents, and all I can do. My work can be to focus on what people eat to improve their health, or what they wear or where they live and so on. So, my purpose has given me the work I am supposed to do.

LIFE IS GIVING

About 10am in the morning, a young boy was flipping through a newspaper his father had just brought to the house about an hour ago. He was one of those typical kids who were always fond of comics and cartoons inside newspapers and magazines. As he was turning the pages, his prying eyes stumbled on one of the headlines that stated that a young boy, who was of his age was murdered because of his fight against child abuse and slavery. This happened in South Asia. The name of the young boy who died was Iqbal. Iqbal was sold into slavery in South Asia when he was four years old and was chained to a carpet-making machine for good six years, where he was toiling day and night. It was a terrible experience for a young child like Iqbal. Later on, he escaped and began to raise alarm everywhere of how children were being mutilated and dehumanized by some wicked group of people. To a sad end, Iqbal was killed to stop his campaign for freedom for children. This stirred up anger in the young boy who was reading the newspaper. "We must continue this fight", he thought to himself. He hurriedly cut a portion of that news from the newspaper and put it inside his school bag. He had made up his mind to figure out what to do. He wanted to show that children have power as well and they could fight as long as it takes, knowing that *a bravest voice could live inside the smallest body.* The following day, he showed it to his classmates, and they were shocked as well. He asked them if they could join hands with him to fight the cause, and not to allow Iqbal to die in silence. Promptly, eleven kids had shown their interest, and that was the beginning of a group called "Free The Children" movement. It was like a joke, together these twelve kids began to inform everyone around them. They told their parents, siblings, friends, and friends told their friends and teachers and everyone around them. In no time, it became an anecdote and the news circulated everywhere where these young kids were. They raised funds and got massive supports from different organizations to help those children in slavery to give them freedom and education. Furthermore, they connected with other children in many of those affected countries and began to raise awareness, with support from companies, organizations, and different associations. They created their own education and development programs. Presently, the group is one of the largest networks of children helping other children through education in the world. They build schools, provide clean water and health care, and fight against child abuse and slavery. The young boy who was reading the newspaper then, and initiated this whole process is now a grown-up man, but he still continues to commit himself to that cause he started when he was twelve years old. He flies all over the world, helping children, and creating awareness against child abuse and slavery. The name of the young boy was Craig Kielburger.

LIFE IS AN OPPORTUNITY

We often hear opportunity comes but once, meaning it's only one time we have a big opportunity in life. Perhaps there may be small other opportunities, but the big one only comes once in a lifetime and once it's missed, that's all. This is not true. Life itself is an opportunity, in fact, the greatest opportunity. The good news is that we all have it. We don't need to start looking for it. If you are alive, it means you have it. So why is life the greatest opportunity? Life is the greatest opportunity because it's from it that we are able to do everything. If you've got plans to go to school, marry, have children, help people, do something and so on, it's because you are still alive. For someone who is dead, there's no plan or future ahead of them. The only thing after death is judgment. No one asks the dead what their plans are. They can't even talk with them. They've got no plans. But as for us who are still alive, there's a lot we can do here. Every time we open our eyes to see the light of a new day, we are being presented with a new opportunity. Opportunity to live a good life, make better decisions, work in fulfillment of our purpose, achieve our dreams, get new ideas, meet new people, bless new lives, help new people and so on. Life presents us with all that we desire out of it. It's now our choice to decide what we actually want out of it, by going for it. We will not sit down and be waiting for an opportunity to come, because we've already been presented with the greatest opportunity. But we will go ahead and do what we have to do. We will start that business, we will launch that project, we will meet that person, and we will go to that place. Everything we want to do, we will get them done because we are alive, we have the opportunity.

LIFE IS A CHOICE

Life is a choice. You either decide to live or not. We've heard cases of many people who have terminated their lives. They committed suicide. Some even engaged medical practitioners to help them with it, we call it Euthanasia. When somebody is tired of life and gets fed up with everything that is happening around them and feels they have no solution or way forward, they decide to terminate their life. but as sad as it is, different people have got different reasons for doing so. Life is a choice. It's a gift that has been committed into our hands. We could decide to use it or not. We were given to live and make impact with it. people who have not come to understand how precious their life is and what they are living for would find it easy to terminate their life, even in the face of difficulties and challenges. Though there could be hard times, they are not meant to pull us down, but to build us up. Our attitude is very important to how we live our lives and respond to life situations. The choice we make every time will determine how our life will turn out to be. Some people have made wrong choices that have pushed them into where they are. And then now, they want to make the final choice of terminating their lives. So, it was small choices that accumulated into big ones and they ended up terminating their lives. God has given us good choices to make in life. He wouldn't want us to take bad ones because he knows how the end will be. Therefore, to live and enjoy a good life, let's make good choices at every time. Pay attention to what you do every day. How do you spend your time? What do you do every day? What choices do you make every day? Are they good or bad choices? You know for yourself when you make a good or bad choice and you can see the results of those choices you made. Learn from those small choices you made so that it will prevent you from making wrong big choices. Study and learn from the word of God. I see your life being guided and instructed by the word of God.

ESSENCE OF LIFE

We have examined different aspects to life. But what is the essence of life? Imagine you gave someone a thousand dollars to buy five items for you. The essence of that money is to buy those five items. Let's consider scenarios in which the person didn't fulfill the essence of giving that money. First, if the person bought less items. Second, if the person bought more items. Third, if the person bought different items. Fourth, if the person didn't buy anything at all. Fifth, if the person bought all the five items but didn't deliver them to you. None of these scenarios fulfilled the essence of giving the money. Each of these scenarios is applicable to what happens to us as humans. Imagine the person who gave the money is God, and the money is your life, and the person who is asked to buy the items is you. Which of the scenarios best fits your position now? You know quite alright that you were given a thousand dollars, (your life) but do you know the five items you are supposed to buy with that money? If you do, how many of them have you bought, or you are still keeping the money? There's a time limit to keep the money before time is up. So, start discovering what those five items are, and begin to buy them. You can only know those five items from the one who gave you the money, God. And those five items are the essence of giving you that money. Remember, God is happy when you buy those five items and deliver them to him. He gives you the money and decides what items you should buy with it. As you go through this book, you will find more clarity and direction in knowing those five items, and your life would be lived to its fullness because you would have discovered its essence and purpose.

LIFE AND WORK

Let's define *work*. Most times we are used to common definitions. But let's define work like this- an *activity or performance directed towards getting something done.* Our world is filled with work done by people. We wouldn't be where we are today if not for work. Things wouldn't have got this better if some people had not engaged in work. Work makes life work. So, what's the essence of work? First is to keep us living. We are living because we are working. The moment we stop working, we stop living. How does work keep us alive? Right from inside, our body organs and cells are working every time to keep us alive. Let's look at things around us. You know we need food to live. But food doesn't fall from heaven. Some people produce it. The farmers work to plant crops and rear animals. When they are due for harvest, they are turned to food by man. Imagine if there are no people who are planting new crops every year, hunger would have killed every one of us. But because some people are working, we can eat food and stay alive. What about where we live, some people worked to put the structure in place. What about the materials we use, our clothes and shoes that protect us from cold weather, our electronic gadgets and lots and lots of many other things that we use? If we didn't produce these things by ourselves, some people invested their time and energy and worked to produce those items. If other people's work benefits us and keeps us alive and even enjoy it, the least we can do is to reciprocate as such so that other people can also benefit from our own work as well. Enough of a selfish and consumer mindset that dominates the hearts of many people. "If I have money to buy something, why should it bother me how they produce it, or what hell they went through?" It should bother you because if they didn't produce it, your money cannot serve the function of what you bought. If you bought a car, your money cannot drive you if there's no car to buy. There's so much value that comes out of the products of our work than just chasing money and thinking everything is all about money. As important and essential money is it has its own place and functions. Work indeed keeps us alive. The second thing we want to look at when it comes to the essence of work is what we become by virtue of work. Work makes us grow and mature. Life is not boring because of work. If you see anyone who always complains about how life is boring, ask them if they have work. I don't just mean a job or anything to just keep you busy. I mean work. Remember the definition of work- an *activity or performance that is directed towards getting something done.* You see that it's not just any activity, it has to be directed towards getting something done. It means it must have a result. There must be an end goal to every work. So if you are doing something right now, check if it's directed towards an end goal. Find out if you will have results at the end of the day. It's not just enough to be busy with doing something, we must make sure what we do is directed towards getting or achieving something. That's work. As you go through this book, I implore you to look into every area of your life and begin to work on what needs to and you will see change in your life.

CHAPTER 3
MY DISCOVERIES AND RECOVERIES

"Here's what I've discovered about life that; Life is predictable; the way you plan your life is the way you will find it. Whatever you invest or put into yourself is what you'll become. If you work hard or dedicate yourself to something in life and believe in yourself, you'll have results, believe me!"
Abiola Olojo, in a discussion with Sam Owoeye.

In my few years of living, close to three scores now, I have discovered some things in life, part of which I'll like to share with you. You know when your life is in God's hands, there's no longer mysterious events in your life that you cannot demystify or the so-called difficult questions that you cannot answer. Everything becomes illuminated under the light of God's word, *for God is light, and in him is no darkness at all. I'm also the light of the world* and therefore, there's no darkness (confusion, unsolved problems, difficulties and so on) in my life. Then in reality, life becomes easier, not because problems became lesser, but because wisdom became greater. Here are a few things I've discovered about life.

ABIOLA OLOJO

LIFE IS PREDICTABLE

Growing up, I wouldn't believe this- *"life is predictable."* How? We had always been taught life is mysterious and whimsical. It happens anyhow and you don't know what will happen to you. You don't know whether God will help you or somebody will hate you. It's always by luck or by fate. Nothing is predictable. You can't plan anything. I don't mean change will not happen one way or the other. Even if it does, you have a way to control it in the direction you want, because it is inevitable. It happens anyways. With the wrong mindset, it's easier to believe that there's absolutely nothing you can do. You just wait to see which direction your life will go. There's nothing you can do about the government or the condition in your country. You just believe that God would solve all the problems and if He does not, there's nothing you can do. These and many more were the *'deadly mindsets'* I had growing up. But when I discovered that life is predictable, *I realized that I can plan my life and predetermine what will happen to me.* I am where I am today because of what I did or didn't do. Nobody is responsible for what happens to me, except me. It was a shocking revelation coupled with mixed feelings of why didn't I know this much earlier in my life. But anyway, it wasn't too late for me to begin to organize my life and plan a better future, and with the understanding that my life is already in God's hands, it's a victory-assured life. I have the assurance that I will live my life in health, wealth, peace, joy, abundance and all the good things of life if I will only follow the principles that guide these things. This is what we all have access to, as God's blessing is for all of us.

TIME IS LIFE

This is something we hardly pay attention to but very important. I've heard time is money, but how is time life? if I'm supposed to live 100 years on earth, and I have lived half of it, it means I have 50 remaining. Let's break it down to seconds. Fifty years is just 600 months. Six hundred months is 2400 weeks. Two thousand four hundred weeks is just 16800 days, and sixteen thousand eight hundred days is just 403200 hours, and four hundred and three thousand, two hundred hours is just 24.2million minutes and twenty-four million, two hundred thousand minutes is just 1.45billion seconds. Imagine a second that is less than 2 billion, how long do you think that would last? That's why we must make sure every second of life counts. Pay attention to what you do every day because those are the things that will amount to something for you in the future. The future is not far, it's here. Do what you have to do and start doing it now.

LIFE IS NOT FOR THE WEAK AND LAZY

If you are a weak or lazy person, you will not make

a good life, because life is not what you sit down and expect good results from. Most of the things we don't plan for will happen in life. If such happens, what will you do? Part of preparing for the future is to gird up your loins and believe God is there with you to help you overcome anything and everything. Being the best-selling female pop singer of all time, with over 200 million albums sold, and one of the richest women in the world of entertainment, you would think that Celine Dion has had an itch-free life. But no, she did not. She was born into a family of fourteen children, and she was the youngest. Her family was so poor that they had to struggle to eat and put on decent clothes. She had to learn the value of things and manage resources from an early age. Her big family provided her with love and encouragement to pursue her music and be committed to it. She started out with a homemade audio tape she made at age twelve, and her career as a singer and songwriter brought her to the spotlight in her native province. She had to work hard to learn English and perfect her show-business skills before she could break into the broader world music market. At the beginning of her career in 1989, she nearly lost her voice. She injured her voice box during a concert and was told she might need some medical attention to speak properly again. Initially, she was frantic, but later surmounted courage and held on to good expectation from the situation. She was put on weeks of rest, therapy, and a new regimen of practice and technique before her vocalization was restored. After many years, she reached the height of her popularity, and many awards were given to her, with gold records in both English and French covering her walls. She produced a lot of hit songs among which was the one titled "My Heart Will Go On" (used in the hit movie Titanic) which made her a world sensation. But in her private life, she had issues she's dealing with- she hasn't had a child and her husband was diagnosed with cancer. She made a decision to leave her career for some time and focus on her family. She nursed her husband back to health with lots of care and support, and she went for fertility screening so that she could have a child. Eventually, she did. She gave birth to a boy in 2001. And after a while, she successfully restarted her music and produced more albums and a series of sold-out shows in Las Vegas. After her many years of fame and popularity in the world of music, she remained top-notch and influential, and her songs remain some of the best songs of all time. As a Goodwill Ambassador for the United Nations, and a multi-million-dollar contributor to health and education charities, Celine Dion helps other people overcome their life challenges and gives them support in whatever way she can. In addition to her life blessings, in 2010, she gave birth to twin boys. And that's what could happen to a life that is determined to succeed and make meaning out of life.

LIFE IS NOT A MYSTERY

This is against what religion and culture have taught me. There were certain events that happened in the past that I thought they were mysterious. In all of those things, there was always spiritual connection; things like attacks from the enemies, living in abject poverty, premature death, undiagnosed protracted sickness and so many negative occurrences that could portray spiritual wickedness. But when I understood that many of these things have come out of how our minds have been conditioned for negative things, I refused to agree that life is a mystery. We feel the devil's presence more than God's presence. Even normal events of life, we'll say they are spiritual attacks. Somebody would say poverty is a spiritual attack when they've not learned the principles of how to become rich. Or another person would say premature death is an attack from the enemies when they've not found the cause (and that most times it's not related to any enemies but wrong mental conditioning). And for someone who lived a purposeful life while on earth, death is not an attack but a transition. Many things that we think are mysterious are things that knowledge would solve. The truth is that *we remain in darkness when we don't have knowledge. Knowledge is light. It discards all darkness. The more knowledge you have, the less mystery you experience in life.* God didn't create mystery. Man created mysteries for themselves. The bible says *God is light and in Him there's no darkness at all.* If there's darkness or mystery in your life, it means there's no God, because God is light. And there's no mystery in light. Mystery is darkness. It is something unclear, cloudy or difficult to solve or understand. That's not God. That's darkness. We have to come out of darkness and all these wrong ideologies. Remember we've been brought out of darkness and have been translated into the kingdom of light, the kingdom of God's dear son, Jesus. We're no longer in darkness but in the light. Therefore, walk in the light.

LIFE DOESN'T END HERE

Perhaps, you've imagined how things will look like when we all leave here and the world comes to an end. How will things be? Where will I be? Will I still be able to recognize myself and all the people I had known? These and many more questions you might have, but the bottom line is that there's life after leaving this earth. All our works and labor will not end here. If you've been a blessing to people, and you've been giving help and support to those in need, count yourself to be among those who will receive reward from God. See what Jesus said, *When I was naked, you clothe me, I was hungry, you fed me, I was thirsty, you gave me something to drink, I was a stranger, you took me in, I was sick, you visited me, and I was in prison, you came to me.* Then the people who have done all these things will come and say, *Lord, when did we do all these to you, but we never saw you for once?* And he will say to them, *in as much as you have done these things to the least of my brethren, you have done it to me. And he will ask them saying come, ye blessed of my father, inherit the kingdom prepared for you from the foundation of the world.* For those who didn't do all these things, they will have their portion in the lake of fire, where the Devil and his angels will be. Imagine by just being a blessing to people and giving support to those who are in need, God will reward you abundantly. What a nice deal. This is not just about the acts. This is coming from a heart that loves and cannot put his eyes off helping those who are in need, or support for those in difficult situations. If you can understand how much people appreciate those who give support to them when they are in need. How much more God, who will bless us with great rewards. I've once been in dare moments of needing help, and I know how it feels. People who came around me at those times are always in my heart and I can go to any length to give them support as well. This doesn't mean I don't help other people. I help everyone around me and those who I know are in need. But to tell how important people appreciate our help when they are in need using my own experience. It's really noteworthy. And the amazing thing is that the need for help never ends, people will always need our help and support, even to the least person among us. It may be moral, financial, psychological, physical or even spiritual support. All help (whichever form) is important, and God appreciates them all. Go ahead and give that support. Blessings are yours.

SETTING PRIORITY IS IMPORTANT IN LIFE

There could be many things for us to do. Different things may be calling our attention here and there. But only one thing is needed. Doing many things at the same time is putting our strength and energy in many places, it wouldn't yield good results. For absolute results and productivity, we must focus on one thing. This wouldn't mean we won't have time to do other things. It just means we have to set our priority and do the needful first before we go to other things. By the way, what have you found out to be the most important thing in your life? I don't mean you should tell me, God, because God is everything and we're all for him. Something connected to your purpose here on earth. Can you summarize it to just one word or phrase? This will help you to know what you are living for and be able to stand for something. People who are highly successful are people who have specific areas they are specialized in. Their purpose and priorities are defined. They are not jack of all trades that would be master of none. It's important we define our purpose and set our priority in life because we don't have luxury of time and can't afford to waste any of it.

GOD IS REAL

This is not a religion. It's an experience. I discovered that God is real, more than what religion or anyone has ever told me. I believe there's God in heaven, and I believe all the things I've read in the bible. But you know the experience you have when you move from theoretical knowledge to practical knowledge. That was the encounter I had. After the death of my husband, I was in deep grief and sorrow. I wouldn't know what the future would look like. Fear gripped my soul and I cried day and night. In the midst of all that, I encountered God. Streams of joy and hope flooded my heart like never before. I was able to touch heaven and felt the heart of my heavenly father. It was an experience like no other. This was the first time I knew God as a father. I had the confidence that a child has when he knows his father is there with him and for him, and enemies are making noise outside. No shaking. My fears and worries disappeared. I could literally ask and tell my father anything. I feel he's with me all the time. I don't pray or fast religiously like I used to do before out of fear. Because I now have a better understanding of his presence with me. His love and compassion compassed me about, and I wondered what kind of God I had claimed to know ever before in my life. It was a great and powerful experience for me.

WE'RE EXTENSIONS OF GOD'S LOVE

God didn't just create us in his image and likeness, he created us to express and manifest his nature. And that nature is love. Love is expressed in one word- giving. You can give without loving, but you can't love without giving. It is the nature of God that brought the idea of making man in his image and likeness, after he has made all the beautiful creatures. None of them would have been capable of receiving God's love, even though they are also products of His love, but not an extension of his love. The difference is in the creation. Man, because he's the mirror image (selfie) of God, he has the ability and nature of God and can effectively communicate with God at His level. Other creatures were not in the image and likeness of God, and so they can't communicate with God at His level. When I discovered this, I realized I was supposed to be an extension of God's love to my fellow human beings. As God has shown His love to me, I should also reciprocate that to His people. I can't claim I love God if I don't love people, because humans are objects of God's love. So whatever love I claimed to show God must be expressed to people; their race, religion, gender, culture or traditions notwithstanding. Nobody is exempted from God's love. I realized that people can be loved, appreciated, celebrated, and forgiven if something unpleasant happened. I learned that the best of man is man. And being a man, he's limited by flesh and mortality. But God in man makes him unlimited and wonderful. So, I will always trust God in every man but not in man himself.

YOU CAN CREATE YOUR OWN WORLD

Oftentimes when we look at what is happening around us, the havoc, evil, calamities and all the troubles that are besieging nations, we want to lose hope and become pessimistic about the world. But the truth is that you can create your own world which will affect the entire world. Out of all the bad news we hear, there is still good news. Out of all the evil, we still see good. There are people who are making an impact daily in our world. They are doing great things that affect humanity positively. Such people are not disturbed inside. They are not affected by the negativity outside, but they are always creating positive things inside that will bring positive change outside. That's how great nations are made.

YOU ARE THE ONLY THINKER IN YOUR MIND

Do you know you are the only thinker in your mind? I know most times we hardly think about that. We are always in that continuous loop of thinking about people, things, and different occasions that are associated with us. In your mind, there's no other person there with you. You are the only one. This gives you absolute freedom to decide on what to think. Many people think freedom is outside. But true freedom comes from inside. Your ability to decide what to think in your mind every time. This is very important. You've heard, a*s a man thinks in his heart, so is he.* It sounds simple, but doing it is hard work. How do you decide on what to think when there are so many thoughts flooding your mind at the same time? Researchers told us that the human mind processes at least 50,000 to 60,000 thoughts every day. That's more than enough for execution. This is where true freedom is exercised. You want to exercise control over your thoughts. I remember there are times when my mind would be cumbered with so many thoughts. What I do in those moments, is to streamline my thoughts to one thing. I would ask; which one thing do I need to do now? I will work on it and do the rest later. If I don't do that, I could be there thinking from morning till night without achieving anything. I understood that my mind is an important tool that God has given me to create my life and future. I know the days when I'm worried, I would become so reckless and found it hard to sleep and eat good food. But the moment I allowed peace, I saw the difference. It's good to allow and keep good thoughts in our minds, despite all the negative things around us, because it is the good thoughts that we keep in our minds that will bring us the good life that we want to enjoy on earth.

I SHOULD BE OPENED TO PEOPLE'S LOVE

I discovered this; people's love is amazing. There are people who have the heart of God and always want to express God's love to other people. They are so kind-hearted, genuine, humble, and supporters of good things. They will always be there for you in the times of trouble, as much as they are there for you in the times of celebrations. They are people whose God's love has been shared abroad in their hearts. You'll know it's not your money they are looking for, or to seek special favors, but from a genuine and loving heart. They are people who want our lives and humanity to be better. They contribute to the environment and our world in general. They are people who are keeping everywhere lively and healthy. They are such loving people. I thank God I have those kinds of people around me and their good hearts have rubbed on me, and I reciprocate the same heart to people. In as much as we are trying to show love to other people, there are people around us too who want to genuinely show us love as well, they want to give us their time, energy, resources and every other thing they have in their capacity to give, let's be open to their love. People don't like when we are cynical or skeptical about them. We should show good attitude to everyone and give them the benefit of doubt if we have any issue in our heart. It's always good to love and be loved by people.

I DISCOVERED MYSELF AND MY JOY WAS FULL

There was a day in my meditation time I was going through a scripture, in one of Apostle Paul's writings to the Thessalonians. It came so alive in me that I couldn't believe I had ever read that scripture before. It gave me the exact picture of who I'd wanted to be and do for people. Here's the scripture; *"Finally, when we could stand it no longer, we decided to stay alone in Athens, and we sent Timothy to visit you. He is our brother and God's co-worker in proclaiming the Good News of Christ. We sent him to strengthen you, to encourage you in your faith, and to keep you from being shaken by the troubles you were going through. But you know that we are destined for such troubles. Even while we were with you, we warned you that troubles would soon come—and they did, as you well know. That is why, when I could bear it no longer, I sent Timothy to find out whether your faith was still strong. I was afraid that the tempter had gotten the best of you and that our work had been useless. But now Timothy has just returned, bringing us good news about your faith and love. He reports that you always remember our visit with joy and that you want to see us as much as we want to see you. So, we have been greatly encouraged in the midst of our troubles and suffering, dear brothers and sisters, because you have remained strong in your faith. It gives us new life to know that you are standing firm in the*

Lord. How we thank God for you! Because of you we have great joy as we enter God's presence. Night and day we pray earnestly for you, asking God to let us see you again to fill the gaps in your faith. May God our Father and our Lord Jesus bring us to you very soon. And may the Lord make your love for one another and for all people grow and overflow, just as our love for you overflows. May he, as a result, make your hearts strong, blameless, and holy as you stand before God our Father when our Lord Jesus comes again with all his holy people. Amen." This scripture opened my eyes to a lot of things. First is the love and responsibility I have over God's people. And this is not limited to people of my faith, but to as many people that need my help. The love of God has been so shared abroad in my heart that I cannot just overlook people in pains or afflictions. This scripture also gave me the picture of how people can be vulnerable to danger if they are alone and don't have support or care from anyone. Sometimes, I have a burden in my heart to talk to someone and when I do, I see how they are in need of help and care at that moment. At times, I don't know whether I have problems or not because I'd have been so concerned with people's situations that I can't remember mine anymore. I realized this is my nature and I can't run away from the responsibility. Some people find it amazing how I could do what I do even with a lot going on around me, and I still have time for people, and I would say in my heart, *this is who God has made me to be, and*

I'm grateful for it.

SUCCESS IS PROGRESSIVE

Success is not just a one-time event. It's a lifetime process, from one level to another. This would mean there's no final destination to success here on earth. If you go to school and you acquire some degrees, you celebrate the levels of success as you progress. So the success is in the progress. When you keep moving forward, you'll keep making success. Some people complain about challenges and problems. They just want everything to be the same, no change. But they want success. But there can't be success without progress. And there can't be progress without tests. Just as a student can't have progress without exams or any form of assessment. So is every one of us. And the truth is we'll all face the exams of life. Those who pass will progress, those who fail will try again or fall back, depending on their decision. Life is fair enough to those who understand it. There's no point complaining when you are not seeking out a solution. If you are ready for success, you will look for a test to write so you can pass and make some progress. I remember when I was in college, exam time is what every one of us always looks out for. Because that's what will determine our progress to the next level or graduation. So I always make sure I pay attention to preparing for it, so I won't fail and come back to write the exam. Alas! Sometimes I failed and had to rewrite the exam again before I progressed to the next class. I see this happening in life. Many of us, the challenges or difficulties that we dodged sometimes in the past and failed to face and overcome them are coming back to us now. Because until we pass that exam, we will not progress to the next class, and therefore no success in view. Perhaps the situation you are going through now might be the exam you need to pass before you can progress. The success you are looking for is in overcoming that challenge. Don't look sideways. Face it upfront and you will overcome it. Sometimes we wouldn't know how less difficult something is until we do it. Start to do it and you will see that you can do it. See this; The temptations in your life are no different from what others experience. And God is faithful. He will not allow the temptation to be more than you can stand. And when you are tempted, he will show you a way out so that you can endure. This is a great word of assurance and confidence. There's nothing you have gone through or going through that's beyond your capacity or what you can handle. Therefore, surmount courage and take your victory over that challenge.

NO ONE CAN KILL YOU

Yes. You read that right. No one can kill you. Jesus gave us understanding into this. People can kill your body. But they can't kill your spirit. They can damage your body. That has got nothing to do with your spirit, because you are not your body. spirit that lives in the body. Imagine what Jesus said, *"Don't be afraid of those who can kill the body but cannot kill the soul. Rather, be afraid of the One who can destroy both soul and body in hell."* It's only God who has the power to destroy life because He's the creator of it. But you know what, He would not destroy it. He's so gracious and kind. He's your father and creator. Sometimes, humans threaten themselves with death. Some people have lost their peace, joy, and comfort because someone threatens them with death. Jesus said forget it, no one can kill you. Because you are more than what any human being can kill. You are God's spirit clothes inside the body. So there's no need to fear death or threats by men. If you are God's spirit, you are god. If nothing can kill God, nothing can kill you. As a matter of fact, when God was creating you, he put immortality inside of you that cannot be mortal, no matter what. Our presence here on earth is temporary. We will transcend to eternity where we will reign with Christ. But it's important for us to do what we are here for. There's a need to accomplish our mission here on earth. And that would be a prerequisite to enjoy good rewards. So, go ahead with your work and do what you are brought here for.

GOD DID IT PERFECT, YOU MUST WORK IT OUT

Some people would say, oh why am I not lucky?

Why didn't God favor me like that person? Why are all these troubles on my head as if God is angry with me and several other bothering questions like those? But God has done a perfect job over every one of us. No one is unfortunate as far as God is concerned because he always creates time and chance for every one of us the same. See this scripture: *"I returned, and saw under the sun, that the race is not to the swift, nor the battle to the strong, neither yet bread to the wise, nor yet riches to men of understanding, nor yet favor to men of skill; but time and chance happen to them all."* Take note of what is common to all of them, time and chance. Each of the statements in that passage is powerful. As against what we are used to, let's consider the first contradictory statement; the race is not to the swift. In other words, someone can have the talent of running 1 kilometer under 10seconds, but that doesn't mean he would win the race. Or someone who knows how to fight might not win the battle or someone who is a professor of mathematics might be begging for bread. So what determines who succeeds in life? Is it by luck, favor or talent? Or maybe God is angry or happy with some people? The answer is in that passage- *"but time and chance happen to them all"*. Let's note the words- *time, chance* and *all.* Time and *chance* is what God made available to *every one of us* and those are the only determining factor of anyone's success or greatness in life. Not by favor, not by luck, it's *time* and *chance*. What is *time*? It's what you have right now. It's the moment you are having with me right now. You might have one thousand and one things you wanted to do, but you decided to read this book right now, and have my thoughts and ideas shared with you. That's your time you are maximizing, that's the value you are adding to your life. I'm sure there is one or two wisdom in this book that would bring remarkable change to your life if applied. That's your time, the time that you have and every other person has, that makes all the difference. What about *chance*? It's within the spectrum of time. It's very momentary. Once in a while, once in a blue moon kind of opportunity. Life itself is an opportunity. But there are some moments in life when opportunity is at its peak- we could call such a moment of *chance*. Just imagine the way we use the word- *chance*. You can say you give someone a chance to do something or use something. The *chance* there, is an opportunity available only at that moment for the person to use it. If the person didn't make use of the *chance*, it will go and the person may not get a second *chance*. But the idea is that *chance* is always momentary and most times might not be repeated. So, have a moment of reflection and meditation, what *chance* do you have right now? It will not always be available. Maybe you've missed some *chance* in the past and you're still regretting up till now. It can really be painful especially if you didn't know it's just a chance that wouldn't last longer than you expected. Don't worry, clean your eyes, and don't beat down yourself. There are better days ahead. Don't let your past rob you of your future blessings by still remembering those negative past and creating negative energy and atmosphere around yourself. Come out of your past and begin to live in the reality of what you want your future to be. The good news here is that there is time. Remember in that passage *time* and *chance* happens to them all. And inside the spectrum of *time*, there's *chance*. You have *time* now to change the status quo, to make things work, to do things better and differently, to forgive that person, to change your attitude and behavior towards people, to begin to work on your long-abandoned project, to resolve that dispute and let the past be past. You have the *time* now. Yes, the opportunity of still being a living soul, to begin to work in the fulfillment of your purpose on earth. Some people buy cars, houses, private jets, yachts, gold, lands, and many other material things that don't give them fulfillment. While those things are good, they can't replace your life. Achievement is not the same as fulfillment. Although, achievements come with fulfillment. So, if you are fulfilled, you will surely achieve. The best life to live is to live for the sole reason of why you are here. Therefore, let fulfillment be your goal.

USE YOUR TIME TO SOLVE YOUR MONEY PROBLEM

What problem do you have right now? Perhaps it's something related to money. You have given one thousand and one reasons why it's only money that can solve your problem right now. I want to ask you something; do you have time? If you have time, you can solve your money problem. You can use your time to make money. We often hear time is money. Just few people truly understand and walk in the light of that truth. How do you use your time to make money? Time is your greatest resource. The first thing you want to do is to use your time to diligently find what problem you can solve around you. What problem do people around you have that you can solve? There are thousands of problems around us, with new ones popping up every day. So, problems in the world cannot be exhausted. After finding what problem you can solve, then think on what solution you can provide. There are two basic principles here; selling of goods or offering of service. If it is selling of goods, you need to understand the goods/product you want to start selling. If it is an offering of service, you'll need to acquire the skill if you don't have it. There you will start learning other skills like human relational skills, communication skills, marketing/selling skills, networking skills and so on. I know for some people, the process may be too long, oh this will take a long time, I need to solve my money problem now. What they don't understand is there's nothing like solving the problem now, as I mentioned earlier, if you want to solve any problem, you need time, and when it comes to major problems like financial problem, you need good time. People who are lazy, who don't want to put in the work or make the sacrifice are the ones who always want shortcut. They want to bypass the process and have the result now. Some may engage in criminal activities to make sure they gratify their desire and escape work. But they don't know that they are either postponing their work or bringing curses on their head. Because when you cheat other people because you want to become rich, the money you got will become a curse. Nothing the money is used for will be successful, because it's cursed money. So, it's better to pay the sacrifice and solve the problem once and for all, instead of looking for shortcuts that would hurt you in the future. I've seen so many people in distress and calamities later in their life, when they've used their youthful days to sow bad seeds and now, they are reaping it in abundance. They would always cry bitterly in regret and shame. You wouldn't want to go that way. *Righteousness exalts nation. But sin is a reproach to any people.*

CHAPTER 4
SEED PLANTED IN HIS HANDS

"When you sow a seed, God multiplies it for you."
-Abiola Olojo, in one of her talks.

'Seed is the unit of reproduction of any living thing, capable of developing into a full-grown structure of that thing.' The idea of seed is for multiplication and continuation of things. If I want anything to multiply, I turn it to a seed. And if I want anything to continue, I turn it to a seed. The future of anything is in its seed. The idea of seed is applicable. Everything that is still in existence in our world today and keeps multiplying and could be metaphorically described as a seed. But seed cannot survive on its own. It has to be planted and watered before it will begin to bring forth fruits and harvest. Farmers understand this very well. They know how to utilize seeds for good harvest. Knowledge and experience have taught them 'where' to plant their seeds, 'when' to plant their seeds and 'how' to plant their seeds. Those three factors are important for good harvest. One can have good seeds, if those three factors are not in place, the harvest will not be good. There are many things that could represent a seed, ranging from tangible to intangible things, such as children,

ideas, projects, money and so on. To expect a good harvest, you will need to plant your seed in God's hands. What ideas do you have today or what project are you working on? Commit them to the Lord so that your efforts will yield good results. It's not good enough to always do everything by trial and error. When you can have a clear direction and instruction of what to do, why do you need to waste your time running around? Many people have been frustrated and got tired of life because all their efforts have yielded no results and they don't know what else to do. In that case, there's still something else to do, submit your ways to the Lord. He knows the beginning and the end of your life. Now, this is not a religious cliché or trying to put your own responsibility on God. It is to understand the source of life. People who have discovered great things in life got them by being attentive in their spirit. They don't follow the crowd. They have quiet moments (in solitude or meditation) when they get direction and instructions on what to do. They follow through until they have results. You also can enjoy this. You can take advantage of the opportunity you have to engage your mind and spirit in meditation and get direction for your life. You've got seeds (in the form of your ideas, plans, thoughts, and children) that you can plant in God's hands and begin to enjoy a bountiful harvest.

CHILDREN ARE GOD'S HERITAGE

Every parent wants to have good children. They want their children to turn out good and be a blessing to the world. They give them good education, home training, and legacy to as much as they can afford. But sometimes, parents face challenges with training their children. Some of the challenges could be financial, environmental, social or ignorance. However, parents are not happy and want to do everything to make sure they get their children back on track. Sometimes the children could engage in wrong activities that could tarnish the image of the parents. In such a situation, it has to be a more committed effort from the end of the parents, involving both physical and spiritual. Talk with them, pray with them, and if needed, consult a professional, like children psychologists or counselors. Though it's always better to put your children on the right path early in life. So that it will be easier to put them back on track if they derailed. Notwithstanding, children are God's heritage. And God cares so much about them, even more than we parents do. He'll help us to train them and show them the right way. This would mean we should take care of them and guide them under the instructions of the Word of God.

MONEY IS A SEED

Do you know money is a seed? You can plant your

money and have some good harvests. We do that in the form of investments. The idea of investment is simply planting your money now and have good returns in future. We know people who are rich became rich essentially because of investments. If you don't invest, you won't enjoy abundance. *Abundance comes from investment.* There are different types of investments; from real estates, to bonds, to stocks, to businesses and so on. There's also another important place we can invest our money to yield a good harvest. It is in people. You can invest your money on educating someone and they become great and bring wealth and abundance to you. You can invest your money on sponsoring a good idea, and it yields a good harvest in future. Peter Thiel invested in Facebook at the early stage of the company. He was one of the first angel investors of the company. He invested $500,000 in 2004, and by the end of 2012, he's already made over $1 billion in cash. That's what you can get from investment. Money is a seed that must be sown. But it's important to know how, where and when to sow it. And that's what you get from knowing how investments and markets work.

GOD DIDN'T PERFORM MIRACLE TO CREATE HEAVEN AND EARTH, HE WORKED

Yes, you read it right. It wasn't a miracle that did the creation of heaven and earth. It was work. How do I know it is work and not a miracle? Let me explain.

What happened in the account of creation in the book of genesis was similar to what could happen to us in any seemingly hopeless situation. Instead of waiting for a miracle, God worked. How? First, when God created heaven and the earth, the earth was void and empty. Darkness was everywhere. Then the spirit of God and the word of God began to work. God used six days to do his work. And on the seventh day, he rested. I think it's someone who has worked that rest. A person who doesn't work has no need to rest. God didn't look for shortcuts even though he could find one, but he did work. So why won't you work? If God our creator, the maker of heavens and earth worked, then we've got no excuse not to work. Jesus said- *My father works hitherto and I work.* I sometimes hear some people say "If you work or labor before you become rich, it means you are under curse or God is angry at you," and I laugh because those people don't know what they are talking about. It's an expression of ignorance about the nature and personality of God. Work is as important to God as his Word. He carries out his word by work. He doesn't release his word and goes to sleep, he accompanies it with work, which makes him to have results all the time. If you know people who just talk without work, then you know you've met people who will not have a result in life. How you know people of great value is they follow their word with work. They always work out their word to make it valuable before men. *As much as words are important, work is much more important if we want results.* God didn't create the earth just by his word, he followed it with work. It's his work that is keeping the earth alive even up until now. That's why Jesus said, *even up until now, my father works, and I work.* Because he understood the importance of work, and it must be a continuous thing. So, in all you are doing, let work be your watchword. To implement your ideas, solve that problem, be financially independent, train your children and so on, all these require work. People who have good harvests in life commit themselves to good work.

DEVELOP YOUR TALENT

There were three people who were given talents. First was given 5 talents. Second was given 2 talents. The third was given 1 talent. The first developed and used his talents, he got 5 extra, making 10 talents. The second did likewise, he got 2 extra, making 4 talents. The third went and buried his talent under the ground. When the master who gave them the talents came and asked them to give a report. The first came and said I've multiplied the talents you gave to me, now I have 10 talents, the master said 'good servant', well done, enter the glory of your father. The second gave the same report, I've multiplied my talents and now I have 4 talents. The master told him too, good servant, well done, enter the glory of your father. Then the third came and said to the master- you are a wicked master, you just want me to work for you without any pay. I didn't use the talent, I just went to bury it somewhere, now take back your talent. Then the master said, *"oh you wicked servant, what have you done?" "You just wasted my time and the value I gave to you. If I had known this is what you would do, I would have put it in the bank to have interests on it. But now, you just collected it without using or investing it. You are a waste."* That's the third servant who refused to develop and use his talent. The first and second servants got more rewards, they were put as heads of governments in the kingdom of heaven. *Whosoever is faithful in little is faithful in much. By principle, God knows that if you do well here on earth with what he has given you, you will do well there in heaven with what he will give you.* There's no need to be running after going to heaven. You don't need to rush to heaven. Make your heaven here on earth. Bring heaven to the earth, don't take earth to heaven. God brought us here to be a blessing to the earth. That's a fundamental truth, whoever you are, notwithstanding. Now you may ask, but I don't have talent, how do you want me to use what I don't have? Every one of us has got talent. The challenge may be with your understanding about talent. Talent here is not in the way many people have put it – something conspicuous that only you or few people can do without learning or training. But talent, in this case, is *everything you've got to be a blessing to earth. That particular value you should add to the earth. That particular problem you should solve. That particular need you should meet. That's your talent here.* You don't need to look for something outlandish or strange that nobody has never got. Of course, you are unique and different from other people. But the idea is you wouldn't need to set your eyes on spectacular things that people see outside but, on the virtues, and values on the inside. Look, check, examine and scrutinize in your closed-door things that you've got on the inside. Can you pay attention to things that you have done in the past? Can you remember the good comments people have given about something nice you did? Can you remember things that always draw your attention, annoy you, or set you ablaze to act or fight? I'm talking about your passions and actions. Things that you could do without anybody forcing, coercing, or even paying you to do it. Things that you know are always on your heart, they always drive you and make you act/behave in a certain way. You may need to pay attention to those things. These are things you love to do. Meanwhile, it could also be things that we are used to as talents such as music, arts, cooking, sports, profession, leadership, medicine, entertainments and so on. There are various sectors and ministries where every one of us can work without restriction by religion. What we have is to bless the world, and not just some groups of people. What we have is for the entire world. *We are the light of the world and the salt of the earth.* So don't be restricted by any religion or belief system that could limit your impact or influence in the world.

SEEKING DIVINE DIRECTION

I remember sometimes ago when I had issues concerning my two sons. It was about their studies in school. They would come back from school, sometimes not do their assignments, play around and go back to school the following day without doing their assignments. And then, their teachers would give me reports of how they were not doing well in school. Then I thought it's high time I did something about this before the situation gets out of control. I had to pray and meditate in my spirit to know what I would do. Then I got a direction, and I went ahead to do it. Eventually, the children changed, and now they have become better people than they were before. Now, they better understand life, people and situations. I was amazed at so much wisdom that was coming out of their mouth. They even told me that they would love to give advice and share their experience with younger people so they would learn from them. I just thank God I took that step. Perhaps you may have a similar problem or know someone who does, the important thing is to ask God for direction on what to do. Not even on this matter alone, but on every matter of life. The methods may be different, but the principles are the same. The principle is to get direction from God. Sometimes He could lead you through another way to solve the same problem. I've heard many parents complain to me about their children for the kind of unhealthy life they live and there's nothing they can do about it. In that situation, I advise that they seek divine direction. *The heart of the king is in the hand of the lord, and as the rivers of water; he turns it wherever he wills.* The *king* in that context signifies *someone of high rank, value, who has authority and control over people and things, it also means someone who cannot be easily controlled or has gone out of control.* But God still has control over him. Let's read that text again, *The heart of the king is in the hand of the Lord, and as the rivers of water; he turns it wherever he wills.* The same way you can decide the direction water will flow inside the tap in your kitchen, that's the same way God directs the heart of a king. Why? Because He's his creator. He's his life. The king cannot breathe without Him. He's the breath in his nostrils. He's the thoughts and ideas in his mind. So, he can't do anything or be anything without Him. So in the case of children who are hard to control, you can get divine direction and that problem would be fixed. And knowledge is important. Seek professional knowledge to understand the stage where your children are in and how to handle the situation with them. Sometimes it may just be to take simple steps and the problem would be solved. I see your children becoming great of the Lord. *"And all your children will be taught by the Lord, and great will be their peace."*

YOUR FUTURE IS IN HIS HANDS

Perhaps you are in a situation where you think nothing will work for you in the future. *"No job, no work, no money, no spouse, no direction. Where is the future?"* I understand. You are down and frustrated. Again, perhaps, the plans you had didn't work out the way you expected, and no one around could help or give support of any sort. It's just blank and dark. Alright, no problem. You got this book at the right time, let me share some things with you. Do you know there's someone who is more concerned about you than you yourself? It would surprise you to know that you are not in that situation alone. There's someone else there with you. I know religion has bastardized spiritual things and understanding about God. *But abuse of food would not make it useless. People still eat food every day. The word of God is a food that we must keep eating for our spirit to stay alive and healthy.* The one who is ever there with you in every situation and He's in your heart. He's the one who keeps you breathing, the one who keeps you walking, talking, and living. You will like to know what he's thinking about you, He said *He knows the thoughts He has towards you, they are thoughts of good and not of evil, to give you hope and future.* So, *He plans your future, prepares it, and sets it before you so you can walk in it.* So, what do you really have to do now? Get to know it and begin to work in it. All of your greatness and glory will manifest to the world.

IDEA STARTED AS A SEED

Alice Waters is a world-renowned chef and creator of the famous California restaurant Chez Panisse. She's a woman full of passion for children and all that goes with healthy eating for young and old people. She specializes in cooking organic food and advocates for its intake rather than synthetic foods that are dangerous to health, especially among young children where there are many cases of childhood obesity. Alice started out as a teacher and was studying education in France when she got an idea of cooking fine food and the fact that organic food, which is locally grown without chemicals, boosts physical health and makes a huge difference in cooking. Back at home, while working as a teacher, she continued studying, cooking, and making delicious organic meals for her friends, and the friends of her friends, and all of the people in her vicinity. They all loved the nice meals. They would gather in her place, having a good time. long enough before Alice thought of opening her own restaurant to serve organic food to everyone. In a few years, her restaurant has grown by leaps and bounds. She had created enough sensation that made other restaurants, supermarkets, and local kitchens around to adopt her ideas for fresh, healthy food. When famous people from Hollywood travel through Berkeley, California, there's only one place to eat; her restaurant. She changed the way that many people think about and prepare food. So, now that she has played a huge role in disseminating the idea of cooking organic food and making it available, she has also decided to use all of her knowledge, wealth, fame, and experience to do something that she strongly believes in- helping children. That's why you'll see one of the world's best chefs going around to schools to teach kids (and their parents) about healthy eating and organic food. It's part of her national campaign to fight obesity and other health problems caused by bad eating habits that people develop when they are young. Her dream is to help everyone enjoy a better quality of life through healthy eating. So, Alice is changing the world through her ideas. What ideas do you have? Don't hesitate to give it a try. Many people have had multimillion ideas, but only to bury them in their minds. Don't do that. *You will not regret anything by trying but you will regret everything by not trying at all.* Start working on your ideas today and see how things will work out. You will have the opportunity to learn, know and understand things better. I see you moving upward and forward.

ALLAY YOUR FEARS

Is it possible to stay without fear? Every now and then we are cumbered with so many thoughts that put fear in us. So how do we allay those fears, talk less of eliminating them? I remember in my 40s when I used to fear a lot. My fear threshold became so low that I literally feared anything and everything. The fear was about my husband and children. I always thought about little things- *"How are we going to do this? How are we going to do that? What would happen after this? And so on."* I became so distraught and frantic. What happened? Nothing. All the things I had feared and became so anxious about just became needless. They weren't as serious as I thought. You know the challenge with us as humans is that we don't usually learn from the past unless it's very serious. The moment something happens, we do it and forget about it. Even the same situation could repeat itself over and over again and we will still express the same fear and anxiety towards it. When it comes to us as women, we are on a different level from men. Every little thing bothers us. We care, nurture, and develop whatever is committed to our hands. We think of solutions before problems arise, we set the table before everyone is ready. That's our nature. We just love to prepare and plan things ahead. We don't like shock, emergency or any bad surprises. They sometimes put us in disarray or preventable embarrassment. So, as for us, there are many thoughts that we nurture in our head in a day. I think that's just the way we are designed. I believe it's a blessing to our world. Now, in my 50s, all my fears have disappeared. I think I found one antidote –to solely depend on the assuring word of God. When troubles and difficulties come, and they want to overwhelm or bring me down, I just use the word of God that I kept in my heart to subdue them. It's amazing how I experience so much joy and peace in my heart whenever I do that. Most times, I also sing and worship. It's really a nice experience for me. I feel burdens are lifted and all pain is gone. Wow! Praise the Lord.

LOVE DOESN'T DISCRIMINATE

Before, love was something I found very hard to understand, not because I'm not used to hearing or talking about it, but because I didn't truly understand it. Now, this is what I'm talking about. When I was so religious, I would think it's only people in my church who would go to heaven. Other people, I'm not sure about them. Again I adopted the mindset of caring for certain people and less attention to other people. Not like I totally disdain other people, but I didn't give them as much attention as I gave to people whom I love. I had always thought God would give me reward for the good I do only to people in my religious circle and ignore the ones I do to the "so-called unbelievers". So, I was in a closed circle, compared to the entire world that God says I am the light of. Then, after a while, something happened and I realized that I'd got it all wrong. The people I claimed to show love were not the only people God created. They were not the only people God showed his love. They were not the only people Jesus came to the earth to die for. He died for every one of us. The Bible says *for God so loved the world, that he gave his only begotten son that whosoever believes in him should not perish but have eternal life. For*

God didn't send his son to condemn the world but to bring everyone to repentance. That's a genuine and unconditional love. A love that doesn't discriminate. If God loves the world, then I shouldn't discriminate but love everyone also.

WORD IN SEASON

We like it when our friends speak good words to us. We want to talk with them. We want to relate with them and spend all night and day with them. That's such a bond and friendship we could create with our loved ones. Sometimes when we are down and have some difficulties, we could just feel like pouring our hearts to our friends and want to hear whatever they would like to share with us. How much more a great friend, who knows us and knows how we feel, and he's always close to us to comfort us and speak his words that would bring peace and joy into our hearts. He will surely make all good if you would allow him. Welcome Jesus.

WHERE PRODUCTIVITY COMES FROM

Productivity comes from practically engaging our minds in solving problems. There are so many problems in our world that are waiting for solutions. Personal problems prepare us for general problems. You may have financial problems. It's preparing you for global financial problems. Principles are the same whether on a small or large scale. There are people who are always complaining about problems. They are not comfortable with seeing or experiencing problems. How will you grow? How will you move forward and make progress in life, if you are always running away from problems? People who understand life know that problems are blessings in disguise and are raw materials for breakthrough or greatness. Imagine if Thomas Edison didn't solve the darkness problem and produce incandescent light, who will know or remember him today? Imagine if Norman Borlaug didn't solve the food scarcity problem by spearheading the green revolution, who will acknowledge him today? And lots of other great inventors of our time. Their names would always appear in the book of history of the world because these ones have done some things that are global and transgenerational. If you want to mark your name in the book of history, you must be committed to solving problems, not just for yourself, but for humanity in general. We are in a generation where religion is taking time and lives of people in some parts of the world. They claim they serve God while it's just activities and entertainments all over, wasting their time and energy. To solve problems, you need time. Time is your greatest resource to solve problems. Some people think, if they have money, they can solve problems. You don't need money to solve problems, you only need time. And even if you have a money problem, time can help you solve it.

ABUNDANCE MENTALITY

This is the hallmark of prosperity and higher living. Some people would say *"there's poverty in the land. There's not enough to go round. All of us can't be rich. Poor people would never end in the land"* and all sorts of things they talk about. But all these are expressions of poverty and lack mentality. They are good alibis for people to remain poor and continue to manage and endure lack. There's always abundance and there will always be abundance everywhere. How true is it? I will show you in a moment, look around you, there's air, though you can't touch it but you can feel it. Is it in abundance? Yes! Our world cannot be short of air, otherwise, all of us would die. What about plants? Science is still yet to discover many species of plants that exist, after the hundreds of thousands of the ones they've already discovered. What about animals, those on the land, on the trees, inside the water and in the air? Definitely, we can't finish naming and discovering all of them? Are they in abundance? Yes. What about lands/soil, water, natural resources, minerals, and all the biotic and abiotic components present in our ecological earth, they are just too numerous to mention. But is there a lack in our world? No. Lack only exists in the minds of poor people, not in reality. Because all that we can see in our nature is abundance. There's no way the human population can increase that can fill all the space on earth. There's an abundance of space everywhere. What about energy that drives life and makes things work? It's just too much. From solar, to wind, to hydro, to nuclear, to electromagnetic, to sound, to mechanical and so on, there is just too much abundance of energy in our world. You would think there's really a lack in our world until you begin to study nature and understand how much resources the creator has put on earth for the blessing and enjoyment of mankind. Whatever we've had so far are just the result of our work. It shows how far we've worked. Not all that is available. If there's no water to drink in a place, does that mean there's no water in the world? If there's no food to eat, does that mean there's no longer food in the world? It only means we've not worked enough to produce sufficient food and water for ourselves. Nature has more than enough for every one of us. Then somebody can say, but we need money to get all these things? No, we don't need money. Before money came, people were still living well and had all what they needed. Money was an idea. It's not part of the resources given by nature. This is what successful men understand that makes them detach from money and focus on solving problems for humanity. Like I mentioned earlier, you don't need money to solve problems. You only need an idea, which you generate from having time to think. Ideas come from a developed mind. As you go through this book, implementable ideas will come to your mind, not like the ones that you cannot implement, but the ones that are practicable and achievable in any area of your life. You may need to take notes and work on those things later. Knowledge supersedes money anytime any day. Money without knowledge will waste away, but money with knowledge will always multiply. There's always and there will always be abundance in our world no matter what.

THE MASTER PLANNER

Who told God how to shape the nose or the mouth? Who showed him how to make the heart work, or how to put all the brain cells so they function together? or Who told him how to make man walk on his two legs and animals on their four legs? In as much as all these things are natural, they are designed and planned out by God. We know nothing just happens. *Everything came as a result of a cause which brings about an effect. If we can see the hands of God in the things that we can see, how much more things that we cannot see.* Scientists told us that there are more living organisms that we cannot see with our naked eyes than those we can see with our naked eyes. That's the wonders of nature. It will interest you to know that God has finished planning your life before it started. He has seen the end even from the beginning. *He has made everything perfect in his own time and has set everlasting in their hearts.* Every one of us has got some plans, if not written on paper, at least in our minds. We know when we want to finish school, start working, get married, have children, do some projects, travel the world and so on. We've got those beautiful plans. It's good. However, we should allow God's will to work in our plans. We know his will and purpose for us are always good. Read again what He says; *"I know what I'm doing. I have it all planned out- plans to take care of you, not abandon you, plans to give you the future you hope for."* Did you see that? That's what you've got, because he's your father and takes care of everything that pertains to your life. So, live in this understanding and I see you moving from one level of glory to another.

VALUE YOUR WORDS

Words are seeds. The words that we release, whether good or bad, are sown as seeds that will bring forth harvest for us. From now, mean every word you say. It may sound simple but requires continuous conscious effort. You can have a good time with people and make them happy with your words. It's good. In that case, your words are not mere or empty words. But they are substances that add value to people's lives. Many people have appreciated me because of the good words I spoke to them. They told me my word came to them right on time. It was actually what they needed at that time. I was always stunned at those statements, because for me, it's just normal. I mean it's just natural for me to appreciate, encourage, advice and support people. My words are just expressions of my heart to them, trying to share God's love and goodness with people. For me, no one is too small or too big to be loved, or too high or too low. Whether you are poor, rich, young, old, man, woman, white, black, I see everyone as God's blessing created in his image and likeness. I encourage you as well to look at people around you and support them, help them, speak good words, speak sweet words. I know sometimes it's difficult to do, especially when you are in a place where people don't appreciate or show love to one another. But I tell you, you can change the order of the day, you can make things happen. By the time you start with one person, and you do it from a genuine heart, the person will receive it and transfer it to another person. *If people can transfer bad aggression, they can transfer good impressions. If people can transfer wrong things, they can transfer good things.* Be the one who will help people to transfer good things to other people. Remember anywhere and everywhere you are, you are the light. You are the giver, the solution, the love, the joy and the blessing people are looking for. Don't look somewhere else, you are the one. I challenge you today, to start manifesting who you are. You may say, *"but it's because you don't know me, I don't have money, I don't have love, I don't have talent, I don't have anything, what do I have, what can I give people?"* Oh, you just don't know it, you have many things already. Not even what you are looking for, but what you already have. Like I said before, you have love, you have compassion, you have a good heart, you have good spirit, express them through your words. Begin to say good words to people. You can start with saying good words to yourself. Say good words to yourself. Look at yourself in the mirror and see something nice. Encourage yourself. It's not all that bad, there are many good things about yourself that you don't know. You've not seen all of them yet, but they are right there inside of you. Open your inner eyes and you will see them. No matter how small they may appear to be, celebrate them. They are small seeds that will soon become big fruits. They are small plants that will soon become big trees. *Arise and shine, for your light is come and the glory of the Lord is risen upon you.*

GOD IS INTERESTED IN YOUR FULFILL-MENT

No matter how bad we are as humans, we would never let anything that comes from us be ridiculed or denigrated by people. We will always strive to make sure it's something of value that people will appreciate and thank us for. It's always in our nature as humans to make sure people value and respect us because of what we did. Now, how much more God who has created us in his image, likeness and glory. We are his products. He will surely make sure we are fulfilled here and bring us to full awareness of his purpose for us here on earth.

ALL IS AT REST

How I want you to receive that word of hope right now- All is at rest. Over your family, children, job, project, plans, and so on, All is at rest. What does this mean? It means there's nothing left to worry or be concerned about. If it's all, it's all. Nothing left. Can you see how all is at rest? But you want to say, *"I can't see anything at rest, In fact, things are becoming more difficult and challenging. Where's the rest?"* Okay, I will share that in a moment, I got you covered. First of all, you are in the right situation, though you think it's not good, *but it doesn't need to be good, it just needs to be right. If it's right, it will soon turn good.* Here's the thing, the challenges and difficulties are there for you to solve them. When you solve them, you receive rewards? You learn, grow and get better at life. So you want to ask, *"but I don't know how to solve this problem."* You do, you've not just paid attention to it. It's just liked that beautiful dress that you put under other clothes in your wardrobe. You hardly remember you have that cloth until there's need for it and you have to open your wardrobe and search for it. In the same way, you've got so many treasures inside that you have no idea how much they are and could help you with solving problems. Look inward and bring out those treasures. I see you breaking grounds.

SOMETHING IS CHANGING BUT SOMETHING IS CONSTANT

There are many things around us that are changing and there are things around us that are constant. In science we call some things variable factors and some other things constant or fixed factors. Variable factors are always changing, they are not stable or static, they are dynamic and are always influenced by both external and internal factors. But fixed or constant factors are never changing. They are never influenced by any factor. For instance, things that are influenced by time are variable factors, they are always changing. Human body is always changing, from things that we can see that happen outside our body to things that we cannot see that happen within our body. Scientists have shown us through the use of specialized microscopes that things are always going on in our body. Our body is a big multistructural system that has many changes going on inside. Our heart beats every second, our brain receives information every moment, metabolisms go on in our body every now and then and so on. That's what keeps our body alive and keeps all the cells and tissues functioning. It's what makes us grow and develop into maturity. Take a look at your immediate environment right now, many of them, if not all of them are subjected to change. Why? Because they are all products of time. Okay, let's flip to the other side, and consider things that can't change. Are there things that are never changing? *Yes, there are.*

When you open your mouth and make a statement, the moment the words come out of your mouth, you can no longer change it. You can release another word to change the meaning of the words you first uttered, but you cannot change the words you first uttered. This is very important. Words are powerful and they are essentially constant factors that affect everything about life. And that's why the word of God is powerful and affects all things because it's the origin of all things. And it's also laws and principles of God. So, it doesn't change. If you apply the unchanging word of God into your life, it will bring change in your life. Sow the word of God into your life and you will reap the harvests.

THINK OF WHO YOU WILL GIVE ACCOUNT TO

Perhaps your parents can ask you to help them do something, or maybe somebody or your boss at the office. If you accept to do the task, you will report back to them on how the task was. Think about this, if you were asked to give an account of how you've been living your life, what would your answer be? And for real we will all give account of how we live our life to the one who gave us the life, God. This is not in any way to put pressure on us. This is to help us make meaning out of our lives and live a purposeful life. For many of us, there are always distractions; what we will eat, what we will wear, how we will buy cars, houses, and properties, how we will marry, have children, go to school, secure a job, make money and so on. As much as there's nothing bad in planning and achieving all these things, there's need for setting our priorities right and knowing what we are living for. It's just like a common saying- *Eat to live, never live to eat.* Eating and living are important. But one comes after the other. The first statement; *eat to live,* makes us set our priority right as to the fact that living is more important than eating, so we should only eat because we want to live and the other side of the coin is 'living to eat'. On this, we found out that the priority is wrong. If all the reason why somebody is living is to keep eating, then the person has downgraded their life to just food. And as much as food is important for life, it's not the only thing we do in life. It's a fuel that drives life processes but there are things that must be done in life that are not associated with food. That's the exact mistake people who prioritize money and other mundane things as what they are living for are making. Life is not all about making money, or marriage or buying houses and cars and other mundane things that will perish here on earth. Our focus should be on more important things, while we use all these things as vessels, tools, or instruments that can make us achieve faster, easier and better. Somebody who has money has an opportunity of reaching out and helping more people than someone who does not. Therefore, living a purposeful life is the hallmark of fulfillment in life.

TAKE EXCUSE OUT OF YOUR LIFE

One of the things that can never be exhausted in life is excuses. It will always be available. *"I don't have good parents. I wasn't born into a wealthy family. Nobody is ready to help me. Our government is not good. I have worked and worked, and nothing has happened, what else do you want me to do again?"* Perhaps you are doing the wrong work and hope to have a good result. But that's still a way to generate good excuses. I know you can say oh, it's a reason. It's not an excuse. As much as it doesn't bring good results, it's an excuse that should be avoided. When we give ourselves excuses, we cut down on our ability to do something well. We put our brain in that stagnation mood of not making progress, because we give excuses of remaining where we are. Positive change is practically impossible in the presence of excuse. We may know the right step to take, know the right things to do, but all these excuses we generate in our minds will pull us back, they will prevent us from taking right actions. Unless we deal with those excuses first and take them one by one out of our life, success and progress may be a daydream. No one achieves success while indulging in making excuses. Excuse is an enemy of success. *The more excuses you create for yourself, the less tendency you have to be successful.* Take excuses out of your life.

CHAPTER 5
OVERCOMING ANXIETIES

"Many times before, I've become so worried and frantic, even down to every little thing. But now, I've found peace and joy; for the joy of the Lord is my strength."
-Abiola, in one of her revealing moments

I remember the days when I was working on getting a new house, we wanted to downsize and move to a smaller place since my husband is no longer alive and most of the time the kids are away. My head was cumbered with worries and anxieties. Ever since I had never done this kind of transaction alone before. We bought three houses when my husband was alive. I would be there with him, and we would check and sign all the documents. I wouldn't have to bother myself with too much scrutiny since I know he was such a man capable of doing it. This time around, I had to take the bull by the horn and do all the necessary. I was going here and there, looking for better and cheaper options we could go for. The kids were of great support and I was carrying them along as everything was going but at a point, I just felt tired. I had always thought it's a simple thing while we were doing it then. I didn't know there were a lot more involved then than I knew. The stress wasn't so much for me to handle, thank God for good people around me, including my friend and her husband who were of great support. During that time, I would lie down on my bed, rest my mind, and put everything off my head. Most times then, I don't sleep long, I sleep between 11pm and 12am and wake up by 4am. I hardly sleep for more than five hours. I wake up, do morning prayer, clean the house, and sometimes prepare food if I don't keep any in the refrigerator that I can take to work. And by 6am, I'm already set for work and on my way. There are times when I wouldn't feel like going to work. I would feel like just staying at home and resting more. I would try and carry myself to work. The moment I'm at work, I would start feeling better and before you know it, I would become so active and alive. Then in the whole situation, I realized that all I had worried about turned out good. Not because I worried about them, but because I was able to take the right steps towards solving those situations. I'm someone who worries a lot and feels concerned about every little thing. I remember when my husband was alive, he would sometimes say, *"why am I worried about all these things, they would resolve themselves."* I would say in my mind, *"this man is always care-free and doesn't know what's going on."* Little did I know then that worries wouldn't do anything to solve the problem. Now, I don't mean we shouldn't be concerned about problems, but we should head on to solving them without worrying about them because worrying is not going to do anything than making us become more vulnerable to negative outcomes. Though I understand for we women, it's part of our nature to always be concerned and think a lot about many things, especially for our family; children, husband, extended family, and even our work, finances, friends and whatever social or religious groups we belong to. Notwithstanding, worries can be directed to more profitable things like to help us take the right steps on time, remind us of the things we need to do, and become more efficient with our problem-solving skills. One of the reasons why we women are smart with the ability to provide solutions on time is that we would have thought about those problems over and over again even before people come to us. So, when they come to us and we provide solutions promptly, they are always amazed at our shrewdness. That's our nature as women. God created us to be a blessing to our world.

TIPS ON OVERCOMING ANXIETIES

I'll like to share some tips with you on how to overcome anxieties. They are things that have helped me and I think they can help you as well. I know challenges come to us practically every time, and they are usually accompanied with worries and anxieties. In order to live a stress-free life, here are some tips;
-Know the situation is temporary and won't last

long before you'll get over it.

-If there's something you need to do about the situation, go ahead and do it, and hope for the best.

-Have time to rest your head or just lie down on the bed and sleep if you can. If you are not feeling sleepy, you can just remain laying down on the bed.

-Try to engage yourself with something you love. You can talk with any of your loved ones.

-You can go for window shopping or a long walk alone or with someone, depending on how you want it.

-You can get a nice dish, perhaps different from what you are used to, to have a new experience.

-You can listen to music or sing your best songs.

-You can have some moments to pray, meditate and make good confessions.

-You can also have some moments of creating good memories and atmosphere for your loved ones.

-If you like sports, go for sports, like swimming, tennis, basketball, football, or video games, indoor games, gym or any sort of recreational activities of your choice.

DON'T PUT PRESSURE ON YOURSELF

I know sometimes we are pressed to take action. We're forced by everybody to do something. And this tends to overwhelm us and cloud our judgment from taking the right decision and action. Perhaps there's pressure on you to go marry, and start your own family, or to go look for a job, or to go do that thing that you don't really want or ready to do. But all these are just pressure from outside that if you are not careful could raise the pressure inside, and you'll begin to put pressure on yourself. Now, here's the thing, no matter how much pressure you receive from outside, don't put pressure on yourself. Don't rush into doing something just because people want you to do it. If you did it and it brought bad results, you will face the music all by yourself with nobody partaking from it and it'll be full of regrets since that's not what you wanted to do. So, no matter how much pressure you receive from outside, don't let it disturb the peace inside. Don't put pressure on yourself. Stay calm in your mind so that you can think effectively and productively.

WHERE THE KINGDOM OF GOD IS

Some people sometimes were confused, they said *"we've heard a lot about this kingdom of God and how great it is. But where is this kingdom of God?"* Jesus gave the answer to that question. He first said where the kingdom of God is not, that many of us focus on. He said the kingdom of God is not here or there, but is in you. In other words, *the kingdom of God is not outside of us, but inside of us.* Many people today are being driven by what they see outside, the news they get from outside, the direction and instruction they get from outside. But they fail on the way, because they are not from the inside. The kingdom of God is right inside of us. What is the kingdom of God? *The kingdom of God is not wining and dining, but peace, righteousness, and joy in the Holy Ghost.* It means the kingdom of God is not just for pleasure, fun, and all manner of mundane and trivial things that are for the moment that a lot of people look after these days. But it is qualities of eternal life; *Peace* in the midst of life challenges and difficulties, Righteousness in the midst of corruption and human pervasion, and *Joy in the Holy Ghost* in the midst of troubles and unhappiness in the world. There are people who are already living in the kingdom of God while on earth. We don't need to wait until we go to heaven. We can enjoy the kingdom of God while we are here on earth. If the kingdom of God is in us, it means God wants us to enjoy His kingdom while we are here on earth. There is a difference between the kingdom of God and the kingdom of heaven. The kingdom of heaven is a location. The kingdom of God is an atmosphere, a description of where God lives and abodes. If God lives in us, then his kingdom is in us. It makes sense. Some people doubt if God is in them. They say *"I've never heard God speak to me." "I've never done something spectacular that people will say yes, this is God working through you." "And I've never had any conviction whatsoever that God is truly in me, so how can I be sure His kingdom is in me."* Okay, so let's answer the question this way. Do you have life inside of you right now? Your answer will be yes, because that's why you can open your eyes and read this book, that's why you can talk and do everything that a living soul does. Good. That life inside of you is a breath from God, which is God. The life inside of you right now is an indication that God is inside of you. What keeps you alive is from God and is God. So, you should never doubt the presence of God in you as much as you are still breathing and have life inside of you. That life is the life of God. f therefore the life of God is in you which is God, the kingdom of God is in you. To connect to that kingdom and start enjoying its blessings, you need to acknowledge the presence of this kingdom and connect with the spirit of God inside of you. The spirit of God doesn't need to talk in a special or strange way that you are not used to. He can speak through your thoughts, ideas, impressions, feelings, and expressions. So you wouldn't need to wait for one strange voice to start talking to you before you know God is talking to you. Whatever flows and follows the direction of the word of God is from God. That's why to know God you must know His word, know what he can say and what he cannot say. His ideas, thoughts, mindset, and laws are all found in His word. He's a God of principles. If you know His principles and ways, you will not be confused with whatever things you hear. Let the kingdom of God begin to manifest in you through your thoughts, ideas, and mindsets that you have and will begin to manifest in your actions, emotions, and expressions.

AGAINST ALL ODDS

There was a story of an old woman that I found so intriguing. Her name was Anna Moses Grandma, but people called her *Grandma Moses* because she lived so long that she saw her grand and great ground children. She died at age hundred and one. She was one of the oldest people in the twentieth century. She started her painting and artistic works when she was seventy years old. She had ten children and had to go through all the stress and rigor of nurturing and growing up children. Even when her children grew up and she became grandmother, she was still very active, even till she became great-grandmother. It was all amazing to everyone around her of her strength and agility. She lived in the little town of Hoosick Falls, New York where she was doing her lovely embroidery. At a point, she was attacked by arthritis and it was making it more difficult for her to do her needlework, but she wouldn't let that pull her down. One time, she wanted to make a Christmas gift for a postman. So, she went ahead to paint him a picture. The postman loved the painting. And many people wanted to buy most of the paintings that Anna has done. She had been giving her artwork away to friends and relatives. When she could no longer bear the demand, she started selling her paintings for two to three dollars each. In 1938, an art collector who happened to be passing through the town where she lived, saw some of her paintings for sale in the local drug store. He bought every one of them, contacted her, and bought every painting she had at home too. Surprise, surprise! Her long hard work had paid off. Within a year, three of her paintings were included in a show at the famous Museum of Modern Art in New York City. Galleries and collectors started talking about this amazing new artist who captured rural scenes and people in a delightful folk-art style. It didn't take long for Grandma Moses, as everyone would call her, to become famous. Showcasing of her work was staged in major galleries and museums across the United States, and then in Europe and Asia. Everywhere that her paintings were shown, record crowds came out to see and buy them. Grandma Moses took it all in stride. She said something profound; *"starting a new career in your seventies and being active in your nineties just required a positive attitude."* She kept painting right up to her death at age 101, producing over 3,600 paintings. She was such an inspiration, defying all odds and rose to fame in her old age.

DO THE NECESSARY

Have you ever been pressed to go to the restroom? The pressure builds up until it becomes totally un-avoidable. You either go to the restroom or mess up your body. That's the power of nature that compels us to do the necessary. There's a point when we can easily avoid it. Perhaps we are doing some-thing or on the way, waiting for a better time, but the moment the pressure is much, we can't avoid it. We've got to go ease ourselves. That is necessary. There are also situations around us now that need our attention. Sometimes it's when things have en-sued into problems that we realized we ought to have taken steps long time ago. There are problems we can avoid when we do what we are supposed to do on time. For instance, we know we would al-ways need money to do a lot of things. But to have money, we must create value, (forget about those who use dubious means). The value must come ei-ther in form of goods or services. So, we need time to create that value. There are people who will be waiting for miracles or looking for someone who will help them. But that would not work. *There's no such thing as getting something for nothing.* You've got to have value to offer, if you want value back in return. And that's necessary. The sooner you take that, the faster you get free from worries about money. Those who say money is not important did suffer for a long time. The earlier you learn how to make money and become rich, the better you'll start living a fulfilling life.

LOVE WHAT YOU DO

I'm a nurse by profession and I attend to patients who have respiratory issues. For many of them, we do respiratory treatments that can improve their health condition. When I see them, I want to care for them. I realized this stemmed from the fact that I love what I do. I want to make them happy and have compassion and patience for them. Because of this, many of those children love me and always want me to be around them. Even their mothers perceived this as well. And for me, this is just a normal expression of my nature. I know there are people who are happy at their work because they receive good salary and know at the end of the day it's all for their own good. As for me, I just love what I do. I love to care for people and care for them genuinely, whether I'm paid with a big salary or not. Though it's good if the salary is good. That would be a good motivation as well. What matters to me is whatever I have in my capacity to help and support people, I should do that without so much attachment. My understanding about the love of God has also helped me as well. Because when I imagine as much God loves me and cares for me. I can't but just express that same love undiminished, to his people. And If I, with all my imperfections and weaknesses, could be graciously accepted and bestowed with so much love, then I could go ahead and do likewise to everyone around me.

YOUR LIFE IS TRULY IN GOD'S HANDS

There's something I want to communicate here. Your life is truly in God's hands. This is not a cliché or a religious statement. It's what is applicable to everyone who believes. Your life is not in your parents' hands, neither your spouse, siblings or friends, your life is in God's hands. This makes your success to be totally independent of external factors. In as much as people are important in our lives, they are not our source. Our source is God. People can support us, encourage us, motivate us and help us with things that we do here on earth, but God wants us to understand perfectly where our help is coming from. He's the one using those people around us to be a blessing to us. This doesn't give us any sense of entitlement for support or help from people close to us. Someone might be so angry or disappointed that their parents, sibling or relative is not helping them. But they are not entitled to helping you. They only help you because God wants them to, not just because they are your parents and so it's their responsibility to do it. Humanly speaking, we can say it's their responsibility. But this will make us susceptible to dependency and vulnerability. God wants every one of us to be responsible for our lives. No excuse, no alibis. If people around you are helping you, don't take it for granted and say it's their responsibility. Remember there are others who have such people in their lives and are not doing the same to them. So, thank God for the opportunity you have and make good use of it. If, perhaps, you are on the other side of the coin, that the people you expect are not giving you help or support, don't be angry. It's high time you knew where your help and support is coming from. There are many people here on earth that God can use for you rather than just to depend on one person. I've heard several cases of people who received support from where they couldn't even imagine. I'm actually a living witness to this. Imagine, by God's Grace, I'm currently helping and supporting many kids (not my biological children) to go to school and cater for everything about their living and welfare. I took some homeless children and orphans, living under the bridge to orphanage homes and even helped some people to start off their own businesses, give financial and material support to those who are in need and so on. I know I'm just starting, and still have a lot in mind to do for people because I believe this is why God created me. He wants me to be a channel of his love to humanity. To help those who are in need, to support those who are in difficulties and to give hope to those who are hopeless and helpless. Every time I see people in need, I can't just take my eyes off, My philosophy is *I must do something, no matter how small.* That has ever been my testimony. And I can see the results. How people's lives have so changed. How people have become more happy. Children are doing well. I wonder how little help or support can make all the difference in some-body's life. You should not underrate that help you are giving to somebody; it goes a long way and they will always appreciate you for it because it will al-ways be in their heart. You know when you do good or bad to people, they don't forget. And they will count your blessing before you, perhaps when you least expect it.

I HAVE FOUND PEACE

I have found peace. I have discovered joy. Not like anyone has ever told me. But the one I discovered myself. No wonder the Bible says *the joy of the Lord is my strength.* The joy has to be of the Lord, and not of men. If you get joy from men, you may lose your strength at any time. If your joy is from the Lord, then, your strength is forever. Nothing can stop or frustrate you. You know that feeling that you have that you don't know how to describe or explain it other than to just express it the way it comes. It's a joy that overcomes distress and diffi-culties. It's a joy that subdues sadness. Even when there's nothing to be happy about. You are still glad. That's what I'm talking about. Your happiness is no longer dependent on things that happen outside. But on things that happen inside. And what hap-pens inside? The joy of the Lord. It gives me peace and happiness. My friend, I want you to personalize your peace. It's the one God has given you. If God has given you, no one can take it away from you.

Jesus said, *my peace I leave with you; my peace I give unto you, not as the world gives I have given unto you.* Notice the tense of that statement, it is a Present tense. *My peace I give unto you.* It is not a promising statement or based on conditions. It is free of charge. Now, what makes you enjoy that peace is to believe in your heart that you have it. Another important point to notice in that statement is that *He gives you his peace, not as the world gives.* In other words, the world gives you things with conditions or spitefulness. You know anything people give you, they can decide to take it back, especially when you need it most. That's not Jesus. *He gives you His peace and gives you for life.*

WHAT CAN YOU SEE?

Oftentimes many of us see the negative things around us, the wrong things people are doing, the wrong things in our environment, the bad government, the bad systems and so on. We complain about these things without any desire to bring solutions. However, we can make a difference no matter what. We can bring a change. It's not until we get to a position of leadership or become a politician that we can impart our society. Every one of us has got something to contribute to the system. Let's change what we see. We can begin to see solutions to every problem. If you see someone behaving wrong, don't tag them as bad people, they might still be in ignorance. Try and find a way to educate them if you can, and if you cannot, document your ideas in a book or write it as an article and hope they will read it. It's important we see people the way God sees them; *He sees everyone as his potential children and gives them more grace to come to repentance.* If we think of our past too, we'll realize we've once been in their shoes. We've once lived in darkness. When the light of God came, we became new people. And again, even as we are now, we are growing daily and have not become perfect in flesh. Our perfection is in Christ. However, we learn more patience, love, and understanding with people, so that we can positively influence them and be a good model.

COMMITMENT TO GROW

Just the way we will not be happy if our child refuses to grow. Imagine a 12-month-old baby looking like a 2-month old or a 10-year old child behaving like a 3-year old child, I'm sure we will not be happy and we will surely want to do something about it. That's for a child. What about grown-up adults? The fact about life is we don't stop growing. Though biologically, we may stop growing in height, we don't stop growing in knowledge, experience, wisdom, ideas and so on. I've seen some people who think they don't need to grow. They know everything. Their attitude shows it. When you talk, they already know what you want to say. When you move, they already know where you are going. It seems they are the encyclopedia of life. That's an expression of ignorance. Because nobody is an island of knowledge. The height of someone's knowledge is the beginning of another person's own. Someone may decide consciously or unconsciously to stop growing. This would only end up in one thing- the person will start dying. The moment we stop growing, we start dying. There's no middle ground. It's either forward or backward. No stoppage. There must be a commitment to grow if we want to keep succeeding and winning at life. Commitment to grow is commitment to learn. We want to know new things. We want to learn new things. There's no point in being on one spot for so long. We must keep growing and moving forward. I remembered some days in the past when I was so religious. I would only read my bible and my bible alone. I don't read any other thing apart from my bible. We also hear it in church all the time to read our bible every day and don't let other books distract us, or take our attention. Our focus must be on God and his word, and not things of this world. So when my husband called me to come and watch the news or some educational programs with him, I would always feel reluctant, but still joined him. So that was how it was until I became enlightened that the bible or any other holy books are not only the way I can know God. I can know God through reading other books as well. Then I began to open my mind and search for more knowledge. The result was amazing. I realized that God communicates to us in many ways that's not just the bible. Also, I found out that I understood some things I read in the bible better when I read other books. Now, we need to pay attention to the kind of knowledge we acquire, just as the bible says we should test all spirits whether they are of God. There must be a need to test all knowledge as well if they are from God. You may read or hear something that doesn't go in accordance with the Word or mindset of God. Such knowledge you will discard it because it doesn't go in line with the Word of God. That's why having the truth is the first thing we must do before we go on searching for knowledge because that's what will be our sieve or tester that will select for us good knowledge and discard from us bad knowledge. God created all things and he's in everything. But he wants us to have knowledge of good life but reject knowledge of evil. Knowledge of evil disconnects us from God. Someone who thinks he can just live his life anyhow, he holds account to nobody or he can do evil to his fellow man and go scout free has a bad knowledge. He needs to receive the truth. The truth is *our life is a gift from God and he wants us to use it for His purpose.* That's why he gave us all things according to his goodness and loving kindness. What no man can do for us, he did. So, he wants everything to be to his glory. And we couldn't have done less to what he has done for us and the love he's bestowed on us.

DEVELOPING THE RIGHT ATTITUDE TO PAIN

There are different kinds of pains. From physical to emotional to psychological and even to spiritual. Pain is always uncomfortable. Nobody wants it. But it happens. There's a truth about pain, -I*t tells us that something is going on.* It might be going on in the direction we want or the other direction. For instance, a pregnant woman who is at the point of labor began to experience pain. The pain is a good sign that the baby is ready to come. She will endure the pain at the moment to allow her newborn to come out of the womb. After some minutes or hours, the baby eventually comes, and she forgets her pain because of the joy of seeing a new life. There could be another pain maybe when something is going wrong inside our body, say headache or abdominal pain. The pain indicates something is going on and needs some attention. If it's a headache, maybe the brain is overstressed or the nerves are irritated or there's lower oxygen. In that case, getting a rest in a well-ventilated place or the use of a simple analgesic can resolve the pain and bring the person back to normal state. What about abdominal pain? A lot of things might be going on, depending on the nature of the pain. From blockage or over distension of the intestine to damage of the abdominal organs by infections or diseases. Whichever case, the pain is calling our attention to what is going on so we can quickly take measures to resolve it. Though it's uncomfortable and sometimes annoying. A 5-minute of excruciating pain could make someone lose a sense of life and never remember they've once been healthy before. It could be that terrible. But the presence of the pain could help one to quickly resolve the problem and stop whatever is going wrong inside. Imagine if we don't experience pain, all our body parts would have become damaged, and we would have become close to death before we know anything is going on. There are good pains and there are bad pains. Good pains end up with good results, so we can endure it. Bad pains end up with bad results, so we can reject or quickly do something about it. Either way, pains call our attention and tell us that something is going on, either good or bad. There are moments when we've experienced pain in life. Pain is part of life. We would always experience it. There's a pain of sacrifice and there's a pain of regret. The pain of sacrifice profits us. The pain of regret makes us lose. The pain of sacrifice is always at the moment, but the blessing is always eternal. But the pain of regret is always in the future, and it usually lasts long. So, if you have some pains of sacrifice now that seems like they will never come to an end, don't worry, in a matter of time, they will, and your joy will come and it will be full and eternal.

WHOEVER WANTS TO GO, LET THEM GO

We love people to be around us. We love people

to celebrate and appreciate us. But we would not depend on that. We would not depend on the fact that people cannot fail or disappoint us. Whoever wants to go in their own accord, let them go. Sometimes people who we think will be of help to us, people who we think they will support and stand for us in the days of trouble, they might decide not to be available. They might decide to disappoint us and go away. hat's no problem. No need to be devastated or let down. The bible says- *The Lord is my helper, I shall not be afraid what shall man do unto me. And He's always with me, every time with me, I shall not be moved.* You might expect someone to help you. You might hope things would get better if someone is with you. But that might not be the case. God wants us to relate well with people, but he doesn't want us to depend or put our trust on them. This is not being cynical or skeptical about people or life. It is being wise and doing God's word. *Put not your trust in man. A man whose breath is in his nostrils.* Now, pay attention to that passage, he told you the reason why you should not put your trust in man. First, because his stay is temporary here. He has a mortal body, so he can leave here anytime. There are people who have depended on someone to help them and the person has promised to do so, but only for them to find out the following day that the person is dead or no longer capable of fulfilling his promise. They would be so disappointed and angry, maybe at God or at whatever might be the cause. But God had already told us not to depend on man. This is not that we will always want or expect people to die or disappoint us, but of course, people will die, but the important fact here, which is the second point in that passage is to *understand the nature of man.* Every one of us was created by God. We're not here of our own accord. Somebody brought and kept us here. So, we should not depend on our fellow creature but the creator. The creator is the source of all creatures. So the creator just told us the nature of his creature. He said *his breath is in his nostrils.* He knows where he kept his life. He knows the secret of what keeps him alive. And he can decide to take it. Perhaps, let's confirm this in a moment. Try to block your nose and close your mouth for just 5 minutes. You want to make sure air doesn't get into your nose. You should pause breathing in and out for that time. Let's see for how long you can survive it. Imagine just that alone. I'm sure you can't complete that five minutes before you will start gasping for breath. Wait a minute, does that mean life is in the air that we breathe in. Exactly! Science has proven that to us. Our brain consumes more than 14kg of oxygen every day. So, our life is attached to the air that we breathe in. Where does the air come from? Or who provides the air? The creator. He provides all things and makes all things available to us for our profit. So, it would be wrong for us in a way to just depend on a man whose existence or living is never in his hands but the hands of his creator. We rather depend on the creator instead and not his creature, for the creator is the determinant and giver of all things.

DO WHAT YOU LOVE

Many people would feel the same way Diane Warren did as a young girl. She was this kind of girl who didn't want too many people around her but always loved to be alone, and so was misunderstood and somehow different from everyone around her. She lived with her parents in California. At a point, she ran away from home and later came back. She had passion for music and was always fond of writing songs that expressed her feelings and circumstances. She's so creative and gifted with words. While her mother thought there was no way in what she was doing, her father encouraged her and raised her hope of becoming a great singer and songwriter. With that encouragement, she produced her songs and began to sell them. Her first song brought her to limelight, and she released other hit songs which featured other artists with biggest names in music. People like Celine Dion, Trisha Yearwood, Toni Braxton, and LeAnn Rimes. Her music career stepped up to the next level when her songs began to feature in hit films, resulting in six Oscar nominations and a Golden Globe award for "You Haven't Seen the Last of Me," performed by Cher in the movie Burlesque. She now has a star on the celebrated Hollywood Walk of Fame and has been named Songwriter of the Year six times, among a host of other honors and awards. In all of these,

Diane Warren didn't forget her humble beginning, how she started and the challenges she faced. She used her fame and fortune to launch a foundation that supports music and would help the upcoming young artists who have talents but don't know how to go about it. Her foundation also supports music programs in financially challenged schools, and she helps sponsor contests for emerging songwriters. She did a special song for her father who encouraged her while nobody believed her. She titled the song *"Because You Loved Me"* and that song became one of her hit songs. Almost all of her songs became inspiration to many people and have generated great results in the lives of people.

WORD OF HOPE AND ASSURANCE

Have you received any nice words today? Or maybe you expect one anytime soon? The situation you are in now is such that moment when you need that word of hope and assurance. When you are a little bit confused and distressed and look at the future if there's any glimpse of hope or assurance. It's all dark and gloomy. You wouldn't know what to do. I have a word of hope and assurance for you. If I tell you that there's someone who has run the entire journey of your life from the beginning to the end and has got something special to tell you. He's got something to relieve you of your stress and burden. You were actually born out of him and all that you want and desire out of life, he's got them in his custody. He said, *you should come to him, you labour and are heavy laden, he said he would give you rest.* What is rest? Peace, relief, comfort, joy, wealth, happiness, and all those good things you desire from life. He's been waiting for you this long, and he wished you had known this earlier what he's got for you. He said now is another good time for you to taste his goodness and kindness. *Taste and see that the Lord is good.* He wouldn't want you to worry anymore and still carry that heavy burden in your heart, but he wants you to come and experience his love and goodness. He's right there with you.

CHAPTER 6
EXPECTING THE UNEXPECTED

"Sometimes, we don't get what we want and don't want what we get. And if we get what we want, we think it's normal. If we get what we don't want, we think it's not normal. But God knows the best."

-Abiola, (at early morning hours)

Practically every time, we have some things we expect for the day, or for the week or for the year. It's paradoxical to expect what we don't want to expect, or to prepare for what we are not sure is going to happen. However, miscellaneous is part of life and whether we expect it or not, it will happen anyway. Sometimes this happens in the form of change in our plans, and we know that wouldn't really be what we wanted but did happen. I'm sure you would have had many occasions when something that you didn't expect or prepare for happened. It could be something good or bad. If it's good, you will be happy seeing it and hope for more next time. If it's bad, you will never pray for such to happen again. Such is life. *'Expecting the unexpected'* is a form of preparation, getting your mind set, and your loins guarded with all the essentials. 'Bad' is easier to happen than 'good'. The reason is simple- human minds think evil most of the time than good and since thoughts are things, they will come to pass. It takes diligence to learn how to control one's thoughts and eliminate evil thoughts from one's mind every time. *Expecting the unexpected* wouldn't mean to cumber your mind with negative thoughts or be expecting something evil, but it's more of building yourself, growing more and bringing good out of life in every situation. Remember, *the light shines in darkness, and the darkness cannot comprehend it.*

I NEVER EXPECTED IT

One of the dreariest things I would never expect in my life was the death of my husband. I couldn't imagine it, *my life without him.* How would I do it? I wasn't praying for this and not even comfortable thinking about it. I couldn't figure it out in my head. We were so close. People called us boyfriend and girlfriend. We were always together everywhere. When we went to a party or any occasion, we would always sit together in the same place. People have known us together more than they knew people who just got married, even with all our kids already grown-up adults. That's the power of love and friendship. We just fit each other and were good companions. When he died, for a whole year, I was lost in thought and didn't get myself. I was initially calm but later had several moments of deep mourning and sorrows. But those were the moments when

I had an encounter with the spirit of God. For the first time, I knew God as a father, and I felt him like never before. His love and peace consoled my heart. And I knew him as a loving and compassionate father. I touched heaven. The experience for me was a lifetime.

Here's a side thought I got while putting this book together- *"Some people don't know what it means to lose a loved one. It's very painful that it can put one in a state of vulnerability. So that at this time, you don't want to hurt people. But it's important to take gentle care on how we relate with people 'cos we wouldn't know what they are going through at certain times."*

ADVICE ON MAKING DECISION AFTER THE LOSS OF A SPOUSE/ LOVED ONE

I've got a piece of advice for those who lost their spouse or loved one. I felt I should share this from my experience, and I hope it will help someone. I know it could really be so sad and devastating, especially losing someone who is so dear to our heart. There would be a lot of emotional trauma and distraught. When I went through mine, for the first year I was lost in thoughts, and wouldn't feel like doing anything of interest. I could have one thousand and one thoughts flowing through my mind every day. I lost my appetite for food. I had sleep disorders and could easily wake up because of any little distraction. I would roll left and right on my bed leaping from one thought to another. I had moments when my heart would be so heavy, and I would cry profusely. But I thank God I went through all, with God by my side. I would like to say that *people who are around the person who is grieving their loved one should allow them to grief their loved one. Let them express themselves and pour out their heart. Many of those things are part of the healing process at the beginning stage.* There would be several moments of grieving and mourning. And reflections and soberness. All these are normal and a lot of things would be going through their mind. Health wise, they should be taken care of and allow them to seek medical attention so that they will not end up in depression or any other serious medical conditions. I know losing a loved one can be painful, and they shouldn't feel like it's their fault. Sometimes we might have some feelings of guilt or regret in our minds because of something that happened. That's no problem, we are not under condemnation. *Christ has freed us from every condemnation.* And so the people involved shouldn't put blame on themselves or regret on whatever has happened. They should go through the process with warm acceptance in their heart. At this time, there are different stages and that's why it would take some time to heal. While going through the process, everyone involved should be allowed to grieve the way they want; everyone has their own way of handling the situation. So, it should be without rushing or forcing it. Also, as the person involved, you won't want to make important decisions at this time. So you may still need some time because making hasty decisions about certain things might have future implications. Things like finances, properties, and issues relating to in-laws and extended families should be carefully dealt with. So, before making a lasting decision, one should take time out to analyze every bit of it. It's better to prevent problems now than to start looking for ways to solve them in future.

YOUR PROGRESS MIGHT BE SLOW, BUT IT'S ON

You might be moving slow but you are on track. How do I know? You pick up this book to read. There are thousands of other books you could read, but you chose this one. It passes one message to me – that you believe that your life is in God's hands, and I know you want to learn something from this book that you can apply into your life. I know you have some expectations. It won't be cut short, because this is a piece, I put together to share my knowledge and experience that would benefit you. You are on the track. Though, things might not be working with you because you are not seeing them. Things are working for you because you will soon see them. Life is getting better for you. The situations and challenges you go through will soon become a testimony. There are things you learn as you go through the waters that others will benefit from.

Sometimes the progress we make in life might not be in all of the physical things that we can see, but in the understandings that we have; the lessons that we have learned and all of the changes that have happened inside of us. All these are treasures to the world. They are things that people will want to sit down and hear us to share and talk about, so that they can learn from us and live better lives.

THE LORD IS MY HELPER

The lord is my helper – It means I know and acknowledge the source of my help. As humans, every time we need help. Even those who are strong among us have moments of weakness and need for support. No one is exempted from difficulties and challenges of life. But what makes us different is in the attitude and approach we apply. Acknowledging that the Lord is my helper makes me know where to focus my attention on. It helps me to know I have someone who is available and willing to help me at any time. It also helps me to remove my attention from men. This doesn't mean I don't appreciate men; it only means I know where my help is coming from. Look at this scripture; *"Let your conversation be without covetousness; and be content with such things that you have; for He has said, I will never leave you nor forsake you. So, we may boldly say: The Lord is my helper; I will not fear. What can man do to me?"* The understanding I got from this scripture has given me a different approach to life. Before, I would depend solely on people and when they disappoint me, I would feel so angry and resentful. What I understood that the Lord is my helper, I refused to rely on man. I know it is man that God will use. So, I don't have a bad relationship with man, but I know God is my source and helper and He will always use anyone He wants.

MAKING BEST OUT OF LIFE

Gordon Lightfoot was a singer, songwriter, and winner of sixteen Juno awards. He wrote and performed for over fifty years. His music career started when he was still a little boy and his singing talent was recognized and he started appearing on stage, radio, and television when he became a teenager. Throughout the 1960s and 70s, Gordon had a string of hit songs, recorded by himself and other top stars who loved his songwriting. He broke records with his sold-out concerts at Toronto's Massey Hall. However, behind the scenes, Gordon struggled. In 1972, at the height of his popularity, he suffered a serious illness- Bell's palsy- that paralyzed part of his face. For a singer and performer, this was a serious threat to his career. He fought his way through the illness and regained his health, even while keeping up a heavy recording and touring schedule. For the next thirty years, Gordon continued to record albums, perform concerts, and appear on television. By 2002, he was no longer a superstar with number one hits, but he still had multitudes of fans and his performances attracted enormous crowds. Not long from then, tragedy struck again during a tour in his hometown. There was a rupture of one of the major arteries in his stomach and he was rushed to a hospital by aircraft to save his life. He had five operations and stayed in the hospital for three months. He eventually recovered and was discharged. Gordon wouldn't give up his life and music career. He made a comeback and by 2004, he was recording and touring again. Even a stroke he suffered in 2007 that cost him the use of some of his fingers could no longer hold him back. He practiced tirelessly until he could play the guitar and then went back on the road. After a music career of more than fifty years, Gordon is a member of several music halls of fame, winner of sixteen Juno Awards, and a Companion of the Order of Canada. With more than 200 recordings to his credit, including several gold records, his fellow musicians consider him a song-writing enigma. Gordon has an unending passion for writing and performing his music, that even at age seventy-two, he's still recording and touring with his music.

CAN ANY GOOD COME OUT OF IT?

This might be the question people have asked you. Can any good come out of what you are doing? Your children, family, business, work, project, idea or even plans. You know when people ask such a question and maybe you are not sure of what you are doing yet, that might put some questions and fear in your mind. You begin to consider and re-consider what you are doing or perhaps entertain some thoughts in your mind that could make you sabotage your efforts. People always ask questions based on where they are, who they are, and what they know. All these have got nothing to do with you. If people ask you questions out of skepticism or looking down on you, you wouldn't need to take it personally because it's not about you. This could be difficult to understand. *"How do you mean it's not about me? Are they not talking to me or know something about me, at least? Why should I not take it personally?"* Okay, now here is it. Whoever talks to you irrespective of what they are talking about first of all depends on that person- their mindset and the kind of spirit they have. When people commu-nicate to us, first of all they communicate who they are to us, before they focus on what we are talking about. In other words, communication reveals who people are, the kind of mindset and understanding they have about life. There are people who will al-ways find at least one bad thing in every good thing. No matter how good something is, they will always see something wrong. For such people, you know where the problem is coming from, -their wrong minds. In this case, I'm not talking about people who have a good heart and just like to tell the truth in every situation. For those ones, you will see the genuineness of their heart without hypocrisy. But for those hypocrites, they've got some problems inside that they infect other people with through their words and actions. So, in that case, what you've got to do is to avoid such people in your life and move with people who have good minds. What is important in every situation is your personal conviction. What are your convictions about life? A lot of people can tell you many things, but you will only go by what you are convinced about. So, let your conviction be your confession. Believe in your heart who God says you are and you will manifest all the greatness that is inside of you.

GOD IS NOT AGAINST YOU

It's easier to think God is against you when something unpleasant is happening to you. You could think of many things why God is not happy with you, and that's why evil is befalling you here and there. You hardly had nothing else to think about. Don't worry, you are not alone. Many of us think that way. It's almost like when something we don't like happens to us, that's when we remember God or devil. We either say God allowed bad things to happen to us or it's the devil who pushed us to wrong God. We always find somewhere to put the blame. However, God is good, and his thoughts towards us are good always. You need to let this become your mindset so you will have a good relationship with Him. And He surely wants you to. He's such a loving father than what you had ever known. Connect with him.

WHERE IS YOUR CONFIDENCE?

Confidence is freedom from doubt, fear, and skepticism. It is the strong belief in yourself and your abilities. It is also a feeling of trust in someone or something. In all things, you must keep your confidence. Where? In God. Let your confidence be in God and nothing else. Look at this; *"God is our refuge and strength, always ready to help in times of trouble. So, we will not fear when earthquakes come and the mountains crumble into the sea. Let the oceans roar and foam. Let the mountains tremble as the waters surge! A river brings joy to the city of our God, the sacred home of the Most High. God dwells in that city; it cannot be destroyed. From the very break of day, God will protect it."* Did you see that scripture? You are the river in that scripture whose streams make glad the city of God and God is in you and with you, nothing can shake you. And God shall help you, right early, that is, at every time of need promptly. Wow! What a message. There's no way you will digest this into your spirit, and you will not have confidence. When you study the word of God, it gives you confidence. The confidence that casts away fear and insecurities. Therefore, let nothing take away your confidence because that's your key to success anytime. When you lose your confidence, fear, and defeat set in. There are things that can make you lose your confidence. They all start from thoughts in your mind. Don't entertain thoughts that will bring fear, doubt or hopelessness. And also, the people you associate with. Avoid people with bad minds so that they won't corrupt you and stay away from negative environments. You can create your own environment anywhere you are by carefully selecting what you hear. You can hear many things, but don't listen to everything. It means you will put sieve in your ears to select what you listen to and discard what you don't want. There's too much pollution in the world and if you're not careful you may get polluted. Protect yourself and guard your heart with the word of God, because that's where the issues of life come from.

IT DOESN'T MATTER

It doesn't matter whether people are for you or against you. It doesn't matter whether you are born rich or poor. I say it doesn't matter whether the government in your country is good or not. So, what does matter? What matters is the understanding that you have. *In all your getting, get understanding.* Why is this important? It's important because that's what is going to put light in the journey of your life and take away every darkness. If everybody is complaining, you will not because you have a better understanding. A better understanding of *'who you are'* and *'what you have'*. Take a moment and answer this question genuinely from your heart- Who do you think you are and what do you think you have? If you can answer these questions, you've solved more than 90% of your life problems. But how can you answer these questions without getting to consult your Maker? He's got the answers and ready to tell you anytime. Many people go about life aimlessly and cluelessly. They go everywhere everybody is going, they run rat races, they follow the crowd. They are good examples of biomasses. But every one of us has got our individual life to live without coercion or compulsion from our fellow human beings. We'll all stand before the judgment throne of God and give account on how we all spent our lives. So, understanding of *who we are* and *what we have* will help us separate ourselves from the multitude and give us a sense of living on purpose.

LIFE GETS BETTER

Marie Curie was born in Poland in 1867 to a family of famous teachers and seemed set to have an easy life. But her mother and sister both died when she was a little girl, and her family lost all their money supporting polish independence groups. As a teenager and young adult, Marie, who was extremely intelligent, had to take whatever kind of work she could get in order to feed and put herself through school. She worked as a governess, teaching the children of a rich family, and fell in love with their son. The family would not let him marry this penniless woman. Marie was out of a job again. She finally moved to Paris, where her sister was living, and where some of the best universities could be found. Marie lived in a bare attic, tutoring at night, going to the university in the day, and barely making ends meet. Her luck changed when she met another science student named Pierre Curie. They married and set up a laboratory together; they both love science so much that they hardly ever left their lab. Now Marie Curie's brilliance had a chance to shine. She began looking at radioactivity, which had just been discovered, and set up innovative experiments that proved how radiation came from atoms. It was an enormous breakthrough, and she was still just a student. In the years to come, she and her husband made more discoveries- including the important fact that uranium is not the only radioactive mineral. In fact, Marie Curie discovered a previously unknown mineral that she named "polonium" in honor of her native Poland. Although women were not taken seriously in the world of science in the late 1800s, no one could ignore the important discoveries that Marie cure was making. She and her husband shared the Nobel Prize for Physics in 1903, making her the first woman to ever received this prestigious award. Then, in 1911, she won her second Nobel Prize, this for chemistry. Marie curie became the most famous woman scientist of all time, thanks to her determination and success-achieving spirit.

ADAPTING TO CHANGE

One of the most constant factors in life is change.

Change happens every time, whether negative or positive. It takes effort to make positive change. Whereas negative change happens every time. Part of preparation for life is learning how to adapt to change. Change is what many of us dread. We don't want it. But it happens anyway. So, we must develop the skills that will help us to handle it whenever it happens. Perhaps, over time, you might have learned some of the skills. Our body system is built to adapt to change, as change in the environment happens every time. We have changes in weather, climate, environment, people and everything around us. All these subject us to constant adaptation to change. As time goes by, situations and things don't remain the same. When we understand this, we would know how to maximize every moment and prepare for the next phase. Mental, physical, spiritual, emotional and financial preparations are all important. For instance, emotional preparation can help us to know how to handle our emotions toward people and not to always be reactive. Because people's attitudes will change from time to time, and we need to learn how to control our emotions toward them. Also, financial preparation is crucial. If you have means of making good money now, don't spend it all, practice savings, even if it is little. And when the savings is good enough, invest it, so that you can have other sources of income. And also, plan to have multiple sources of income so that change in one source will not crumble your finances. There's no excuse for failure. Money is a tool that we will always need. I have heard some people complain to me about their finances. They would say; *"Their income is not enough. Government did not pay salary and all of that."* It's because they didn't prepare for change. Times when they were getting good money, they didn't do savings and investments that could secure their finances. Instead, they thought things would remain the same. Now that there's change, they blame the government for their ignorance. One of the mindsets of poor people is to always blame other people for their setbacks. They shift responsibility from themselves so that another person would take responsibility for their irresponsibility. No, it won't happen. Everybody must take their own responsibility and do the right thing. It's important we learn how to adapt to change at every point in life so that we don't fall victim of negative change. If perhaps it happened, it's not over. We can still amend our ways and learn from our mistakes. There are still opportunities ahead of us, that if we maximize and walk according to God's plans and purpose for our lives, we will reign and live an abundant life.

DON'T WAIT FOR ANY TIME, THIS IS THE RIGHT TIME

Perhaps you are waiting for the right time. No time is right except the one you make right. Yes, if you are supposed to do something and you are waiting for the right time, you may be shocked that there might not be anything like right time, because no time will ever be right to do anything. You can always make any time right. We can talk about time and seasons. There's time and season for everything, yes. Who determines the time? It's you. Let's take this into farming. Gone are those days when farmers will wait for seasons to plant their crops. Now, with science and technological breakthrough, everything can be done without waiting for any season. Nutrients and a conducive environment can be created for plants to germinate and grow outside their natural season. Man has found out that he can create everything he wants in as much as he has the willingness to do so. A lot of things that we procrastinate as human beings and push to next time are things that we can do right there at the moment. But probably because we don't feel like doing such a thing at that time, we think it's not the right time. How about we create the right time, all by ourselves. If you wait for the time when you will have money, before you start that project, you will wait for a long time. If you wait for when you will become a millionaire, before you will start helping people, you might keep waiting and waiting for life. If you wait for the right time before you'll start that business, launch that idea, meet with that person, or to start preparing for that important occasion, you may never have the time again. This is the right time. This is when you should do it. Go ahead and do it.

THE BEST KEPT SECRET

You will like this- it's the best kept secret. If you are a woman or you know women very well. You'll know we like keeping and sharing secrets, especially among ourselves and with people that we love. Here is it, the best kept secret. Imagine for a second how big the whole earth is, the people and all the things therein. Also think of the space outside the earth, the planets, the universe and all of the huge structures located in different parts of the heavens. These are handworks of the creator- The God Almighty. Now, imagine how big he would be if you're to imagine him. As big as He is that you hardly can imagine, so he's made himself as small as you hardly can imagine. Think of him residing inside of you right now. And he actually is. How do I know? The breath in your nostrils, the beating of your heart, the fact that you are still alive and reading this book now is an evidence that His spirit that brings life is working in every cell of your being. That's why you are still alive. Imagine having the creator of the whole heavens and earth inside of you. Won't this be the best-kept secret, that God, the creator of all things is now resident inside of you? And if He's in you, so is His kingdom. Now, Jesus said to enjoy life, that kingdom must be a priority. *He said seek ye first the kingdom of God and His righteousness, and every other thing shall be added unto you.* What would this mean? It means-focus on the inside first, develop what is inside first, and bring out all the treasures, and then things in the world will run after you; wealth, people, fame, gold, material possessions and all other things that people run after will come to you because you would have become a magnet. When you develop the treasures inside, you become a magnet that attracts all the good things outside. But a lot of people don't have time to develop themselves. It's activities and entertainment all over. And many complain they are poor, there's no job, there's no money, there's no food, the government is not good and lots of other excuses. But they didn't know that all what they will ever need is right there inside of them. *"What will make you great is not outside of you. It's right inside of you. Stop looking outside. Start looking inside. "*. So, begin to explore the treasures inside of you. Bring the best out of you. It's all lying there as potentials. Put them to work and you will see how you will become a wonder to your world.

EVERYTHING IS FAST

These days, everything is fast. Fast food, fast sex, fast talk, fast work, fast transport, fast internet, fast information, fast miracles, fast money and so on. Everything is really fast. While it has the good side, because it helps us get things done faster and better, it has the downside as well. The fast idea first came from young people who are just growing up and have not understood the reality of life. But now, adults too have adopted the idea. It has become a general logo. If we are in a hurry to do something, or go somewhere, of course there is a need to do it fast or get there fast. The problem here is the adoption of this fast mindset that has encroached into every aspect of our lives. Nowadays we always want to look for shortcuts to get anything done. We look for hacks, recipes, instant results, urgent steps and so on, that we've sidelined the importance of time and patience in achieving any result. There will always be a need for patience. We need time. People who understand life understand the importance of time. *There's practically no shortcut with life and there's no shortcut with time. What we don't learn now we'll learn later.* The steps we bypassed to reach our goal will tell us how well the goal lasts with us. You can see people who suddenly become rich. Don't envy them. The money will soon go back to where it came from. It's simple. hey have not learned how to become rich. They only have the money. They are not rich. To become rich, it takes time. *There's an art of becoming rich.* You don't just jump at becoming rich. It's just like a newborn baby who in a day wants to start walking, talking and doing everything that adult humans do. That's practically impossible for now. Though he can do those things later, he needs time to grow, develop and mature. This is applicable to every sphere of life. By principle, we can't replace anything with the virtue of patience. *Patience is allowing time to work. It is giving time its place without interruption.* Patience solves absolutely all problems. Some situations that we don't understand now, if we could exercise some patience, everything will come to light. And to enjoy good relationships and all of the good things of life, you must hold on to patience. And remember, love is patient, so, be patient with your spouse, children, and all the people around you.

MY LIFE IS A TESTIMONY

I have seen the Lord's goodness and faithfulness. I'm a living testimony of the Lord's goodness. What else can I say? This is what I have. This is my life. I have seen the lord taking me from one level of glory to another. Every time, it's always amazing news of good testimony. I'm not faking it. I'm not pretending. It's real and you can start enjoying this life if you've not. Imagine the kind of confidence that you have when you know that the lord is your helper. It means you are settled for life. it means disappointments and insufficiencies are no longer your story. It also means everything about you is secured, including your future. What else should you worry about? Nothing. Go ahead and face life with this understanding, you will surely come out victorious.

FORGET ABOUT THE ENEMIES

If you grew up in the same environment as mine, where talking about enemies is almost everywhere, then you would know it's difficult not to think about enemies talkless of forgetting about them. Then when you see a title like forget about the enemies, the first question you want to ask is how do I do that? Knowing that every now and then we talk about them. If things are not working, I can easily say it's the enemies that are behind it. If I've not got the promotion, I'm looking for at my workplace or I'm experiencing problems or difficulties in certain ways, of course I don't need a prophet to tell me they are demonic attacks and the whole hell is against me. What more? Lots more, and so on and so forth. Here we go with all those wrong mindsets and ideologies that have shaped our lives and determined the kind of results we've got out of life hitherto. So now, do enemies really matter? Should we think about them? Do they determine how our lives turn out? Are they the cause of our problems? Just in a moment, I will give you simple answers to all these mind-bothering questions. First of all, when God created us, he didn't create us with enemies. He created us independently of any factor or being, and has put our success and all that we will become inside of us. *Nothing outside can influence inside except there's an agreement from the inside.* Nothing from another human being or creature can influence you except you agree with it. I mean this. Let me explain further, your life is designed in such a way that it's auto-function or auto-dependent with all the gadgets that are put inside. Let's consider our minds. The problem many of us have is that we've not really understood yet how our mind works. We think everything is spiritual and influenced either by God or devil and most times devil as we usually think. But this is just the result of how we've programmed our minds. The things that we digest into our minds, the environment where we grow up, the people that are close to us, the kind of atmosphere that we've created around us all decide how our lives turn out to be. So, we are products of what we think. *As we think in our mind, so are we.* And do you know that nothing is true until you believe it? *If you don't believe it, it will never be true for you. So, it is what you believe that becomes your reality.* If you believe the word of God, it will come to pass for you. If you believe the word of the devil, it will come to pass for you. So, what makes the difference? What you believe! Therefore, if you have something you don't want in your life right now, don't say it's the enemies, change your belief and it will change. You must understand the power of your belief. That's what shapes your life and determines the kind of results you get in life.

CHAPTER 7
PEOPLE BLESSING

"We won't know how blessed we are, until we know how people are to us."

-Abiola, (during one of her outings)

Someone once asked me; *"how do you see people?"* I said- "I see them in the image and likeness of God- religion, culture, race, gender, and other factors, notwithstanding." I know some people will want to give preference to some people and give lesser value to some other people. But that's not my mindset. I understand that first of all, God is the one who created all human beings, with no one exempted. He doesn't have a preference. Since he created us the same way, he relates with us the same way. Consequently, this would mean he doesn't love one more than the other. Nor raise one higher than the other. Whatever happens to us on earth is every man's choice. The scripture says *"God is not a respecter of persons"*. It means He doesn't have a favorite. Everyone is His favorite. So, what does that mean? It means that nothing depends on Him as far as relating with us is concerned but everything depends on us in the way we relate with Him and our fellow human beings. He has put the ball in our court to decide on how we want to live our lives on earth. Isn't that wonderful? No wonder God is gracious and merciful. Sometimes we believe that God is the determinant of all things, but He has given us so much power than we would ever imagine. He brought us to his level to be co-creators with him and dominate the earth. And He shares his love equally with every one of us without preference. Jesus revealed this to us when he said, *"God loved the world so much that he gave his dear son that whosoever believes in him shall not perish but have eternal life"*. In that passage, I didn't see that God loved some group of people or have a list of people who were able to meet up with His love list. God's love is unconditional. His love to every one of us is equal and genuine. That consciousness helps me a lot in the way I relate with people. People have done me good, and they've also done me bad. I take no offense for the bad because I understand it's not about me, but about the one who created both them and me. There are times when I really want to get angry and stop doing good, but the spirit of God would tell me if I behave to people the way they have behaved to me, whose daughter am I? Just as he himself makes his sun to rise on both the evil and good and sends his rain on the just and on the unjust. So likewise, should I relate with people without any discrimination or prejudice.

BE OPEN-MINDED

There are a lot of things we can learn from people if

we are open-minded. The factors of religion, race, culture, traditions, gender orientation, upbringing, and other factors tend to make us discriminate and limit ourselves within a small circle of people who belong to our 'club'. Perhaps, one of the most common discriminative factors these days is the factor of religion. If you don't belong to my religion, I don't associate with you. Or if you belong to another denomination or school of thought that doesn't connect with mine, we are not in good terms. Howbeit, we limit ourselves and miss opportunities to learn from people, work with them and positively influence them. If someone has a mindset or understanding that is different from ours, it doesn't mean we should become their enemy. It would mean we can create an opportunity to talk with them and share our ideas. Some of these people that we think are 'unbelievers' are not as closed-minded as many of our religious people. They can listen to us and learn from what we will have to say. At the end of the day, it could even mean we will be the one who will learn more from them. I remembered I used to listen to one popular TV host, and I used to like her program until the day she mentioned 'there are other ways in which you can learn about God, it's not only through the bible'. I waited to see if she made a mistake, but she went ahead to explain. I had already closed my mind. I wouldn't want to hear whatever she wanted to say. What! Being so infuriated from my religious mind, 'How dare you say one can learn about God outside the bible' – I grizzled in soliloquy. Since then, I stopped listening to her, until later I began to understand what she was talking about. I attacked her statement with a closed mind that I didn't bother to listen to whatever explanation she had. But when I opened my mind, I understood her and where she was coming from. I realized there are a lot of things we can learn from people if we are open-minded.

YOU CAN BE A BLESSING

If you believe this, you can be a blessing to people. You can help people. What do you have? You have time, ideas, knowledge, experience, physical materials and other resources that you may overlook. A giving mind is a prosperous mind. There's a story of a young man I'd like to share. His name is Jean Vanier. Jean Vanier believed in helping people, especially the disabled ones. He wanted people with developmental disabilities to live in communities rather than in isolation that they had always been put. When he was thirteen, he wanted to become a naval officer and could have had a successful career. As a young man, he felt something greater was calling him. He quit the navy and began a search for meaning in his life, believing that God had a plan for him. Being the son of one of Canada's governor generals, he had everything available for him and had always got all he wanted as a child. Perhaps, all that would have satisfied him and made him complacent. But he wouldn't resolve with that. When he moved to France, he became friends with a priest in France who worked with the developmental disabled. Then, Vanier was exposed to another world- a world where people were rejected, feared, or ignored because of their mental disabilities. Vanier felt God wanted him to do something to address this form of discrimination and prejudice. So, he bought an old farmhouse. He named it L'Arche (French for *Noah's Ark*) and invited two developmentally disabled men to come and live with him in a real home. Without knowing it, Jean Vanier had started an international movement. There are now more than 130 L'Arche communities in thirty countries around the world and still growing. That didn't happen overnight or by itself. Vanier worked and made up his mind to execute his idea despite the fact that it's unconventional. He traveled around the world, spreading his message that the mentally disabled would be better off if we shared our lives with people who challenge our way of thinking, and show us different perspectives. More so, as these people stay with us, they get better and live healthier by communicating and doing things with us. Leaving people in isolation could be one of the deadliest things that could be done to humanity. God created us in families. The scripture says *He made solitary in families.* That's because God didn't want us to be alone. He wants us to be together, because we need each other. We are all *"broken"* in *different ways*, says Vanier- meaning that we all have difficulty dealing with different issues or seeing ourselves as we really are. He believes living with the mentally disabled helps people deal with their own issues, learn compassion, and become better human beings. For more than forty years, Jean Vanier has gone around the world to inspire others to follow his example. Besides the L'Arche communities, he has helped found other organizations to help people with developmental disabilities and their families through faith and community support, and he has written more than twenty books explaining his life and philosophy. While Vanier has been honored by governments and popes, and has received countless awards and medals, he continues to live in the original L'Arche community in France, sharing his life with the disabled individuals and fellow volunteers he calls his friends.

LEARN PEOPLE'S NAMES

Nobody fell down from heaven. We were all born by our parents. From our early days on earth, we got names given to us by our parents and/or every other person who is related to us. The names we bear are very important to us and we appreciate it if people know our name and call us the way we want. I've had several occasions when I asked people their names and they were so happy to tell me and also happy to hear mine. I realized people like it when you know their name and call them by their name every time you meet them. It fosters good relationships and lovely conversations with people that make our environment grow and endears peace in our community.

VOLUNTEER TO HELP PEOPLE

I've never been tired of helping people, even when I'm physically tired or busy, I'll still find myself doing it. At times, I wonder whether it's a talent or gift. I realized that it's a mindset. I just believe people should not suffer because I'm there. Whatever I have in my capacity to do, I should do it without questions. I've done a lot of things in the past for people that should make me stop helping people or show concern, but the truth is if I'm not there to help, somebody else will show up. God always has a way of helping us even when people we expect don't show up. It's better to put our trust in God than in man. I know how I feel when people who I don't expect disappoint me, so I wouldn't want to show such an unwelcoming attitude to other people as well, not because I'm expecting good from them back in return but because I've got the mind of Christ that gives without conditions. So, I try everything in my capacity to make sure I do what I could do for everyone: their race, gender, culture, tradition, religion, or any other discriminating factors, notwithstanding.

SMILE MORE

I do this a lot; I like to smile with people. In my

interaction with people, I've seen how just a simple smile can make all the difference. Imagine somebody who is down and depressed, having lots of worries and concerns in their heart, and I just showed up with a good countenance, and I saw how the whole atmosphere changed, and the person began to cheer up and happy, and I encouraged them and we went for lunch together after having a long moment of no appetite. Sadness dries bones, but happiness makes bones fat. You can make someone happy today by just putting on that good smile on your face. And science has also shown us that it's healthier to smile than to frown. Smiles make the muscles relax which minimizes aging, freshens the face, burns less energy and keeps people attracted to us. If you do it, do it more and more. You will see how you'll always create that good atmosphere and people will love to be with you.

FOLLOW PEACE WITH ALL MEN

Martti Ahtisaari is a diplomat and mediator. He was the President of Finland, and he has been an avid peacemaker who had been sent by the United Nations to many nations of the world to help resolve conflicts and support international peace efforts. He was awarded the Nobel Peace Prize in 2008. There are many examples of misunderstandings and conflicts that have been resolved, thanks to the wisdom of Martti. Some of the cases are the Catholics and Protestants fighting in Northern Ireland, tensions between Kosovo and Serbia in Central Europe, battles between nations and tribes in Africa, bloodshed in Indonesia, and so on. In all of these cases, the opposing sides were brought closer to peace and understanding. Who would have thought that Martti was destined to be a global peacemaker when he was born in a small village in Finland just before World War II? But as a young man, Martti showed a special talent for languages and for teaching – he seemed to be able to reach out to people and help them understand things. When he took a teaching job in Pakistan, giving English lessons and helping train other teachers, Martti Ahtisaari's eyes were opened to the power of nations to help one another. Upon returning to Finland, he started working for the government, first helping diplomats, and then becoming one himself. That was when his ability to speak five languages and his capacity to see all sides of an issue really began to shine. Soon, he was traveling the world, helping to support international peace efforts. At first, he represented his home nations of Finland, but the United Nations soon recognized his talents and sent him to many parts of the world to help resolve conflicts. Ahtisaari's work was challenging and sometimes dangerous; he often had to persuade armed and angry groups to calm down enough to talk to one another. On one mission in South Africa, he narrowly escaped being attacked by government agents. At one point, he turned from peacemaker to politician and was elected President of Finland for six years. He used his position to work with other nations and urge more international cooperation. Since then, he has continued to work tirelessly for peace, and has created a non-profit organization dedicated to ending conflict. In recognition of his success in helping to end violence and to get opposing groups talking, he has been given many major awards. In 2008, he was awarded the Nobel Peace Prize for his efforts in resolving international conflicts. He likes to point out that conflict is part of everyday life, but so are mediation and the desire for peace. It just depends, he says, on which path you choose to follow. Since we are people of peace, we have decided to follow the path of peace and kindness to all men.

BE PROACTIVE, NOT REACTIVE

There are times when we don't like what is going on around us, people around us are doing what we don't like and we are getting offended every now and then. We are totally pissed off and angry at the slightest uncomfortable thing that people do to it. We wonder whether we are the problem or the people around us. No need to analyze the situation too much, the problem can be solved. Yes, people can do what we don't like. Even sometimes our best friends put their steps on our toes, maybe not intentional, but because we love them, we easily forgive them. Now, the same thing can happen with another person, maybe someone who's not so close to us or our enemy, we react differently. Now, the problem is not the situation, the problem is our attitude towards the two people. We feel less offended with our friend but more offended with our enemy or someone who is not close to us. So what we need to address is our attitude, our way of thinking, our thought process about people, our feelings, emotions, actions, and behaviors that directly or indirectly affect the people around us.

WHAT WILL PEOPLE SAY?

It troubles us a lot- the thought of what people will say. Many of us, consciously or unconsciously we make decisions based on people's opinions about us, based on their words, and actions toward us. We are being influenced and persuaded to do some things just because we have someone around us who wants us to do it. In as much as this is good if the person is good and has good plans for us. It could also be terrible and self-destructive if the person is bad and has an evil agenda. You wouldn't want to follow that way, prevent evil by avoiding people with evil minds. Surround yourself with people of God-mind, people who will be a blessing to you and will always have a positive impact in your life, people who will challenge you to do big things, achieve your dreams and fulfill your purpose. Those are the kind of people you want to associate and have a relationship with. And of course, in this case, you would need the ability to discern people well, not just based on their actions, but on the genuineness of their heart and spirit. Some people are smart with showing good actions, but deep down, they are wolves. They can sacrifice their time, money, energy and other resources to entice you and bring you into their covet, only to wait for you to give in and become vulnerable to them and they will bite you with their poisonous venom. So, beware! Not to be skeptical or cynical with people, but to test all spirits and know the one that is of God.

NOT PEOPLE, BUT YOU

It is not what people do to us that matters, it is what we do that does. Somebody can say something wrong to you, and you feel hurt and sad. But what they said is not for you if you don't accept it. They can say something to you that is not for you. So, you are the only one who has the power to accept what is for you and what is not for you. Yes, you can be angry for some moment, but don't let that bother you beyond that day. Any problem you cannot solve within a day, put it aside or forget about it. You don't want to keep pieces of baggage in your mind. You may have no power over people's actions, but you sure have power over your response to their actions, which in turn, could change their actions as well. Sometimes, it could be an act of ignorance that makes some people do certain things, so a good response from you could change their attitude. And if they don't change, keep doing good. You will eventually see results and have a larger heart to accommodate and keep loving people.

MAKE PEOPLE HAPPY

Our life is given to us to live and enjoy, and not only us, but other people with us as well. Now, if life is given to us, we ought to reciprocate that; to give our life to the service of humanity. That's why we are here. If our life doesn't add value to people, there's nothing we are doing here. We are all created to be a blessing in our world. We're not to seek only our own pleasure, but what will also please and bless others. I know some people say, you can't make everybody happy. But I say, you can make somebody happy. So start from there. Don't say you can't make everybody happy and use that as an excuse not to make anybody happy around you. If people around you are not happy, I don't know who else can be happy. Don't run away from what you can do. Work on it. If you don't know how to love or make people happy, learn it. The amazing thing about life is that we can always get better and become whoever we want to be if we so desire and work on it. life is all about giving and receiving. You receive your life so that you can give it to the service of humanity.

THE ESSENCE OF GOD'S LOVE

God loves us. God gave himself to us. Imagine you give yourself to your friend. It means he owns everything about you. He has access to anything he wants from you. Your time, energy, money, and other resources have their obedience to your friend. If God loves us and gave everything to us, for what? Is it so that we can love him back? That's a normal response and the least we could do. Beyond loving him back is to understand his primary motive. The essence of God's love is for us to take up the nature of love, to become love. God is love. If God is love and we came from him. We should express his nature and ultimately become him as well. We are gods on earth. When we become love, it will just be natural to express it. God doesn't just want us to love him back, he wants us to love people. In fact, that's evidence of our love to him. We wouldn't claim to love God when we hate people. They don't correspond. If we cannot love the people who we see, how can we claim to love God whom we cannot see? We know God is everywhere and created everything, among whom human beings are. So God created all human beings. If God created all human beings, then he wants us to love all human beings without an exception. Are you serious? Yes! "What about enemies, witches and wizards and those people who don't wish me well?" They are also included. We should love them as well. "What about if they come and kill me, whose fault would that be?" "Cos I would rather kill them before they kill me." Oh, no, there's no need to kill them. Let me explain. First of all, you need to understand what love is. *Love is patient and kind; it does not envy, boast or arrogant.*

It's not rude, doesn't insist on its own way, it's not irritable or resentful. It doesn't rejoice at evil but rejoices with the truth. Love bears, believes, hopes, and endures all things. it never fails. As for prophecies, they will pass away, as for tongues, they will cease, as for knowledge, it will pass away. But love will endure forever.

Now, you may say, "but I don't have all these attributes or worse still, none of these." "It must be someone else or God they are talking about." It's you they are talking about. You may not know you have all these qualities until you started developing them. It's just like a newborn who says he can't walk, or talk, or do things by himself or even have all the features that adult humans have. But it's just a matter of time, if he keeps growing and getting good nutrition, he will manifest all of those features. But as it is now, being a newborn, though he might think he can't express those features, the reality is he's got inherent capacity and the nature to express them. Likewise, you wouldn't look at yourself as someone who can't express love to other people. You have the seed of love inside of you. Allow it to germinate and grow, and you will see the new version of you, that will be a blessing to humanity. don't worry about enemies, love is the only weapon you can use to silent them. Don't struggle with anyone. By the way, if someone threatens to kill you, and they are trying all they could to carry out their evil act. Report them to security officers and avoid that person as much as possible. Whoever is coming with physical attack should be dealt with by the law. If not, those who think they can attack you spiritually have failed. Because love is a shield. It's an abode that has all the protection and security. You wouldn't need to bother about those enemies. You should just remain in love. Love wins at all times.

HELP PEOPLE ANYWAYS

Imagine if someone didn't appreciate the good you've done to them or worse still pay you back with evil. How would you feel? This is what we experience oftentimes, and we wonder whether there are still good people on earth, or it's just we alone. If you grew up in an environment where people are so selfish that all what they think about is just for themselves and themselves alone. You may want to react to such behavior either by becoming worse or lose connection/trust with people. But I bet it with you that it may be the devil's trick to shortchange your blessing. I have had several experiences with people in which they betrayed, disappointed or took my money away. Initially, I became so angry and devastated over their misbehavior. But as time went on, I realized that it's not about me but God, who gave me all that I have and has made me to be a blessing to people. It doesn't matter whether they appreciate it or not. What matters is that God used me to meet their needs and be a blessing to them.

Meanwhile, I wouldn't say because God uses me, people shouldn't appreciate the good I do to them because it also shows me the kind of person they are and whether I'm going to do them good next time or not. Appreciation is a good way to show love, acknowledge people, and multiply the blessing or goodness. Lack of appreciation for the good that someone has done literally means the person doesn't want the good to continue.

THE PLAGUE OF SOCIAL MEDIA

The world is closer to us than ever. We are now in a system where everything is at the tip of our fingers. We can touch the screen on our phone and talk to someone in another continent. We can easily meet people from anywhere in the world without restriction or constraint of distance or culture. Everything is closer to us. We can be with our phone or iPad from morning till night and we can easily neglect people around us. We're so much in love with being alone and connecting with our social media that we can no longer appreciate physical communication and interaction with people around us. Internet technology has helped us have the world closer, but on the other hand, it has also separated us from people physically close to us. Consequently, communication and people-relational skills are becoming waned and cases of boredom, depression, and divorce are skyrocketing. As much as we want to connect with people online and know what is going on out there, it's important we don't neglect people close to us and around us. People are blessing us and we must appreciate them. And those who are physically close to us know more about our wellbeing than those who are physically far away from us. This is not to ignore people who are physically far from us as well. It is just to put moderation on everything we do. It's good we appreciate everyone in our lives and don't allow the plague of social media to separate us from both our loved ones and people that we know.

THE BEST OF MAN IS MAN

There are times when we put our trust and expectations on men, especially if they are people close to us. We hold their words so tightly as God's. But failure to do what we want them to do will put us in serious disappointments. We can become annoyed and resentful, especially if we know they have the capacity to do it. So, all our hope and expectations have gone down the drain. But what do you do in such a situation? Jesus made a very important point in the Bible while someone asked him a question. The guy referred to Jesus as 'the good one'. I'm sure the guy is not a sycophant; he's not those who are looking for something good from someone. He must have seen something good about Jesus and how unique his life was even among fellow men. So just to describe him as someone whom he has known and has been studying, he referred to him as *the good one*. But you will be shocked at Jesus' reply. He said *"no one is good except God"*. How does he mean? Is he saying no human being can do good or we shouldn't expect anyone to be good? No, this is what Jesus was saying, he was saying what makes anything good or any man good is not himself. What makes anyone good is God. It's God that makes all things good. So when you take God out of anything, the remnant is not good. So when it comes to people, how should we relate with them to bring out good? It is to see God in everyone and give God to everyone. What is God? God is love. When we give love to people, we give God to them and of course we give something good to them. When we do that, the result would be good. The only key that God has used to solve the problem of the world is love. Love is supreme over all methods and sacrifice. And the only force that is keeping our world up till now is love. Love is simple and powerful.

DON'T LET YOUR MOTIVATION COME FROM MAN, LET IT COME FROM GOD

This is to say, you shouldn't let your motives and why you do things to come from outside. But let it be from inside. Sometimes we wait to hear good words from people before we do good, or even let them behave well to us before we reciprocate. But that would mean our motivation for doing good is from man. People can change, but God can never change. It's better we let our motivation come from God and not from man.

Yes, we can take good words and encouragement from people. That's nice! But that shouldn't be our goal. We should focus on something higher. God has created us for His good works, and we should always desire to do them, with or without motivation from men. If you want to do something, let it be because you want to do it, because of who you are, the kind of mind of Christ that you have, and not because people are good or bad. I know sometimes it might be difficult to do good to someone who treats us bad or tries to do us bad. But because of who we are and the nature of Christ that we have, we would not want to focus on that but to express the nature of God that is in us. People can take us for granted but God will never take us for granted. He will give us reward for all our good deeds. If our actions and expressions are motivated by God, we would not find fault with man and we would not wait till someone does us good before we do good to them. Knowing that God loves and appreciates what we do, He will always make His Grace abound more and more for us to keep doing His good works. Be blessed!